The Masters Review

ten stories

The Masters Review

The Masters Review Volume IX
Stories Selected by Rick Bass
Edited by Cole Meyer, Melissa Hinshaw, and Brandon Williams

Front cover design by Chelsea Wales
Interior design by Kim Winternheimer

First printing.

ISBN: 978--1-7363695-0-0

Printed in the USA

To receive new fiction, contest deadlines,
and other curated content right to your inbox,
send an email to newsletter@mastersreview.com

The Masters Review

ten stories

Volume IX

Dara Kell • Leeyee Lim
• Jack Foraker • Barbara Litkowski •
Charisse Hovey Kubr • Rachel Markels Webber
• Stefani Nellen • Paola Ferrante •
Emma Eun-joo Choi • Stephanie Pushaw

Stories Selected by Rick Bass

Cole Meyer, Melissa Hinshaw, and Brandon Williams

Contents

Introduction

I think we're writing as much as we ever did—that despite the distraction, grief, and frustration of the times as we struggle against the dictatorship we have allowed to spread virally into every aspect of our existence, we keep showing up at our desks. We follow our sentences and our hearts into the darkness that lies ahead but which is not total. Or rather is total but not infinite. There is almost always something ahead.

All of the writers in this year's competition have pushed ahead into the dark, carrying what Cormac McCarthy refers to, at the conclusion of his novel, *The Road*, as "the fire in the horn." All are striving for some light which, if it does not lie just ahead, they seek to create.

In my workshops, I find I'm sometimes as much coach as instructor, so familiar are the entreaties and exhortations I give my students. Drop the adverbs (quickly). Show Don't Tell. Always assume the reader is at least as smart as you are. Specificity is the passageway to the dream. Beware of symbolism; metaphor is so much more interesting. Nature is so often misused as symbol rather than given the free agency, the paradox, of metaphor. There is a whiff of brimstone, an echo of the brutality of possessorship, in symbolism. The old oak tree that represents wisdom and only wisdom: imprisonment! *There, we've got you right where we want you. You will be this way and only this way.*

Symbolism is close cousin to the rude faux pas of overexplaining a thing: it's such bad manners. The reader and writer must arrive at the destination together.

I won't bore you with my longer list of do's and don't's. I bring this up however only to remark and remind us what an utter crapshoot judging is. I do it—judge—enthusiastically, unapologetically (adverb Scrabble double word score), but am compelled also to remind all who submitted a story to remember how narrow my aesthetics are. Truly, after the remarkable "Exchanges," I find myself feeling a bit faint.

It is not my disposition or habit to spend space and time discussing here how the other nine stories could be made stronger. What I would prefer to do would be to roll up my sleeves and set to work with ax and saw, hammer and tongs, to work on those other nine, which, with the exception of "Pirating," were and are all so close to one another, for various reasons: slight missteps or perceived missteps in each that were noticed perhaps only by my hyena's scent for meat, perceived by me (and only me) to be crippled each in one way or another. What all the stories here possess is a heart, an earnestness.

The technical work can be learned. Heart, however, cannot be taught. This is the good news.

*   *   *

Look at the first two sentences of "Exchanges":

"Namibia was my dad's racetrack. I was his copilot." Five words balancing five words—equity and equality, yet difference, distance, conflict and tension.

I am in thrall with this story.

*   *   *

Flannery O'Connor is alleged to have made an apocryphal and self-deprecating statement about her work and how, in moments of accomplishment and/or praise, whenever she might have started to think something she had written was all right, or even better than all right, Faulkner would come roaring down the hill with his locomotive full of various literary freight. And when that happened, said O'Connor, it was time for her to get her little red wagon off the sidewalk.

What delights me about that analogy is the equation of literary rankings with things of childhood. Toys.

Comparison can be the thief of joy.

All of these stories were surely a dream, not a con job, in the minds of their creators. Some have a good bit of the thing I love most about stories, heart; others possess the craft of dialogue, which often works best when understated. Some of the other nine stories' strengths lie in setting, or situation, or voice. There's something to build upon in each of the other nine—something to carry forward into subsequent drafts. Which is what we do, as writers.

Only one of these stories has all of these things, and more, however.

"Exchanges" is a masterwork. The way the unsentimental first-person voice has the faint wounded yet elegant and intelligent tinkle of Alexandra Fuller, and the sass of Lorrie Moore, the heart-ache of a Susan Minot story, and a keenness of observation that would not be unfamiliar to a fan of Joy Williams.

The story and writing is, however, as they say, all the author's.

I'm a sucker for wordsmithing that skates with a one-beer buzz just along the dangerous knife blade of too-much-style, masking the great emotion and sentiment, that stirs, wiggles and writhes just below.

There is nothing that is not beautiful about this story. In a way I had forgotten could happen, when I finished the story, all the hair on my arms, face, neck, leapt straight up, and remained erect for long moments as I performed that time-honored ritual of standing up and walking straight over to a beloved to execute physical delivery of an abject, an artifact, a prize and a treasure, of great beauty and power in an as efficacious and immediate a manner as possible: handing it to her and saying those words, only, *You've got to read this.*

Y'all are in for a treat.

—*Rick Bass*
Guest Judge

Exchanges
Dara Kell

Namibia was my dad's racetrack. I was his copilot. On long stretches he would open his palm to me and say "Lizzie." And I knew to hand him something—peanuts, *biltong*, anything salty—to keep him awake. He would chew hard and grip the steering wheel, and his tendons would quiver and the violet undecipherable tattoos on his forearms would dance their smudgy dance. I would stare at him and try to understand how it came to be that I was related to *this* man, with his expansive face, shiny pink skin, gray beard erupting into sweaty old-blond curls that stuck to his neck, a can of Black Label Beer jammed between his thighs, the rest of the six-pack to his left. My dad, Jono.

My mother waited and watched as I picked my way through carcasses of cars, up to the patchwork brick facade of my childhood home. My baby brother Brandon screamed bloody murder in the back seat. Mom honked and drove off, her black Mercedes sparkling in the sun. My dad was in the kitchen wheezing over a massive freezer, legs spread, khaki short seams straining, full plumbers' bum exposed. The freezer was filled to the brim with animals he'd shot that year: springbok, oryx, blesbok and kudu pink and glistening in their plastic pouches. I imagined him falling in, his flesh becoming in time the same color as the sausages and ribs inside. This made me laugh. He turned around, roaring like a lion. He hitched up his shorts, hugged me and slapped my back, knocking the air out of me. Sometimes, I had to remind him that I was a girl.

"How're you, kiddo?"

I sat at the kitchen table while he made me Nescafé with condensed milk. In return, I provided tidbits that confirmed his theories about my stepfather Gary. I described Gary's white Speedo bathing suit, the way his pubes stuck out the sides. I described the remote-controlled curtains in our new house. How Gary had a little bell he rang to summon the maids to bring more G&Ts. How my mother picked out Gary's clothes in the morning before work, sometimes even a pink shirt. My dad loved that one.

We spent the afternoon packing up the truck. I made a list of its contents: gas stove, two gas canisters, box with cutlery, pots and pans, two chairs, table, one tent (my dad would sleep in the truck), two mattresses, fridge, jerry cans, water cans, minigenerator, dad's truck tools. When I got tired, my dad packed alone and I sat cross-legged in the corner of the living room in front of the only beautiful thing my dad owned: an old, bright blue glass globe left to him by his mother, my grandmother Anzabeth Spies-Kannemeyer. She died before I was born. The story goes that she inherited a tin mine in the Caprivi Strip then squandered the family riches on trips to Paris, Chanel lipstick, and lovers across Europe. The globe was a glimmer of grandeur, a secret message from my ancestors to me. Each country was a different stone. Australia was iridescent mother of pearl, Russia a green sea of malachite, Chad the bold stripes of Tiger's eye. I spun the globe around and around, tapping places I'd never heard of with one finger, tapping them into existence: Guyana, Jakarta, Myanmar, Laos.

That night I slept in my old room, now shared with bicycle frames and metal cogs from something like a mill or an army tank. My dad could have cleaned up for me, but I was grateful for the chaos and the unraveled feeling of life in that house. He hadn't changed a thing. The frilly yellow kitchen curtains my mother had sewn when I was a baby were dusty now. Photos of the three of us were everywhere, as though he hadn't heard the news that my mother had left him.

My dad shook me awake at four in the morning. We rode out of Windhoek in pitch darkness and with dawn, the houses and the gas stations and then even the farms faded away. By full sun we were out on the open desert road. Eventually we'd get all the way up to Epupa Falls. I'd never been that far north. North was Kaokoland, where the Himba lived. I'd never met a real Himba before, only seen them in my dad's old Polaroid shots. I thought Himba women were beautiful, eerie, their hair and skin turned red from a mixture of ochre and butterfat, their arms and ankles sheathed in metal beads like the gauntlets and greaves worn by knights of old.

As I fed my dad *biltong*, he told me about the time he delivered a Himba baby. The mother had gone into labor early, before she'd had time to get back to her village. My dad put her in the back of his truck with blankets and kept her calm.

"She was fifteen," he said. "Younger than you are now."

I shivered and vowed, right there and then, never to have sex again, never to bear children and while I was at it, never to get married.

"She was scared shitless but afterward, she promised to name the baby after me. In secret. So somewhere, in some village up north, there's a Himba kid around your age whose mother calls him Jono."

He winked at me. "Maybe we'll find him."

We arrived in Okahandja at dusk. Streetlights illuminated government buildings wrapped in barbed wire. There were hand-written signs along the road that read, *No Water Temporarily*. We pitched our tent at the campsite and I made a fire. We fried up a massive rump steak and warmed spaghetti and meatballs from a can. Festus, the security guard, walked over and gave us five fresh *mielies* to boil. My dad asked him when the water would be turned back on.

"Okahandja!" Festus replied. "When there is water, there is no electricity. When there is electricity, there is no water."

He laughed, high-pitched like a hyena, and walked away.

A stench wafted over from the campsite's unflushed toilets as we ate our dinner.

I couldn't sleep that night. A song was playing in the distance, just loud enough so that I could hear the melody but not the words. I longed to jump out of my sleeping bag and run to where it came from, where people would surely be laughing and licking their lips with sweet salty life. I wanted to hear that song forever. Sometimes when I'm drifting off to sleep, I think I can still catch the tune.

Morning arrived, cool and dark one moment then oppressively hot and bright the next. Sun seared through my tent making everything glow red. As we left the campsite, a young man approached our truck.

He stuck his arm through my open window, shook my hand and said, "Marco Polo, at your service."

He had a bony face; his cheekbones jutted out when he smiled. My dad insisted that we didn't need any help, but picked him up regardless, and by midmorning they were old pals, drinking Windhoek Lagers in the shed in the middle of town that served as beer hall, marketplace, and nursery. Marco Polo told us that he used to be the English teacher at Okahandja Secondary School before it had closed down. He offered to take us to the new mobile school in the next village, if we would give him a ride back to his own village in return. We agreed.

The road was a dry riverbed. Our truck rattled and yawed, throwing the three of us and everything else—tents, fridge, textbooks, jerry cans—from side to side. My dad showed no fear and whooped with glee as we dove into the hairy dips. Marco Polo clung to the half-open window with both hands. From the back of the truck I watched jagged thorn trees rise and fall. A man on a donkey blocked the entrance to the village. He was wearing an old leather cowboy hat. Marco Polo stuck his head out of the window and shouted something to him that I didn't understand and the man on the donkey chuckled, peered into our car, laughed again, and trotted away.

My dad understood whatever was said and groaned through gritted teeth, "Here we go."

My dad was one of the few white men in Namibia who could speak English, Afrikaans, Oshiwambo, and Herero. That's how he got the job delivering textbooks. He could talk to just about anyone. When they didn't understand, he would put his hand on their shoulder and slowly walk with them, back turned to everyone else, talking in his low, important voice. He would say, "You follow me?" and nod his head until the person he was talking to started nodding their head, too. When the ladies with their coral lipstick came up to him at the Lands End bar, offering "exchanges," he knew what to say then, too. My friends and I knew all about their exchanges. And about how the ladies didn't insist on condoms even though German tourists came through town and exchanged with them left, right, and center.

As we entered the tiny village, women swooped their babies into their arms and ducked into their huts. There was no school in sight. We talked to some men who were sitting under a tree, one of whom was wearing a pink woolen cap with a pom-pom on the top—the kind I imagined American schoolgirls wore in winter. He spoke rapidly and pointed in various directions towards the surrounding hills. Nearby, a woman with legs like dead branches watched us. My dad asked her where the mobile school had moved to, and she spat her tobacco onto his shoe and sat down on her haunches under a tree with two old men. They smoked their pipes in silence.

My dad turned to me and said in a low voice, "I tell you what, I need another *jabuli* after this shitshow." *Jabuli* was his code word for beer.

There was no school anywhere. My dad refused to drop Marco Polo off at his village, which was two hours out of our way. They had a mother-of-a-fight in the car. Apparently my dad had walked in between the sacred fire and the headman's hut— something he would have known not to do. Marco Polo said we should have left gifts—maize meal and snuff at the very least—with the elders as a peace offering. My dad accused Marco Polo of misleading us in order to get a ride home.

I had trusted Marco Polo. There could have been a mobile school there that had moved away to better grazing pastures—that's why they were mobile, after all. We dropped him off where we'd found him. As we skidded away, he shook his head slowly and looked at me with eyes full of pity and hatred, a look of lead, a look that filled everything up.

*   *   *

Each morning, we woke up with the sun. My dad would crack open a beer, clean as a razor cut, and we'd start driving. I drank beer too sometimes. He'd managed to convince me that beer was a more effective thirst quencher than water. After the second one he would tell me to stop. I think it was more out of greed than any sort of paternal instinct. At night we would set up camp and he would fry up thick flanks of meat. Mostly we slept on mattresses out in the open, sometimes next to a river. I'd heard about the crocodiles that sometimes crawled up onto the riverbanks in the middle of the night and chomped people while they were sleeping, but with my dad next to me, I felt safe. I watched the stars through palm-tree leaves that made paper cutouts black against the blue night sky, the river swishing angrily next to us and my dad snoring while I thought about the blue glass globe, spinning, spinning, spinning myself to sleep.

We moved farther north. I took pride in filling out our checklist perfectly. Besides textbooks, we delivered maize meal, pencils, sanitary pads and chalk. My dad got paid per delivery and I knew he could use the money, so I tried to be as helpful as I could be. For a while, when I was around ten years old, my dad's tour business was booming. I hated the red bandanaed tourists who came to our house to sign indemnity forms before they went off on their Great African Adventure. They wore hefty hiking boots when all they were doing, really, was strolling through our dusty towns taking pictures of topless women without their permission, then acting shocked when the women asked for payment.

Since my parents' divorce, the business had fizzled out. My dad blamed my mother, of course, but he also blamed President Sam Nujoma, the hole in the ozone layer, and Cape Town. All those anorexic models.

The farther north we went, the more dilapidated the towns got. We spent more time getting lost, more time looking for the school caretaker, the pastor, the Red Cross lady, the missionary, a dozen people who had agreed to receive our delivery but who were nowhere to be found. When we asked people for help, they looked at us with that look I'd seen in Marco Polo's face, the look of lead, the look that filled everything up. My dad said it was because they didn't want their kids to go to school in the first place. In addition to the supplies we were delivering, we now had to buy gifts in exchange for information, so wherever possible, we stopped at a supermarket and bought tobacco and blankets, tea, sweets without wrappers. For himself, my dad started buying bottles of gin and cans of tonic water as well as his usual six-packs of beer.

By the time we reached Tsumeb, our truck sounded like a tuberculotic toad. It was something my dad couldn't fix himself so we took the truck in for repairs. Wimpie van Zyl greeted us with wide-open arms.

"Well, I never," he said. "The white bushman graces us with his presence."

My dad knew most of the petrol station owners. When we arrived in a new town, that's where we went first. The petrol station was the center of our universe, the nexus of all things possible and impossible.

Wimpie and my dad smoked a cigarette and caught up. My dad fought in the Border War with him, the South Africans and Namibians united against evil: SWAPO, the Angolans, the Russians, the Cubans. Wimpie leaned down to me, came in so close his yellow whiskers almost brushed my face.

"I'll never forget it," he said. "Cassinga, 1978. SWAPO guys shooting at us from all corners, bombs going off, and your father here crawls up under our tank and fixes it"—he punched my dad's arm in time with his words—"right there in the middle of a freaking war zone."

My dad looked at his feet and his pink face turned red. It was one of the few times I had ever seen him look embarrassed. To break the silence, I threw my arms around him, stretched them around his immense beer *boep* as far as they could go, and said, "My hero." He pushed my arms away. Ours was not a family of huggers.

The streets were empty. Most people had gone home to their villages for the holidays, except for some women sitting on the side of the street selling beads, their bare breasts drooping flat on their chests. A woman in a blue dress was bouncing a crying toddler on her knee. She was holding a quart of Black Label Beer. The brown glass bottle was almost half the baby's height. She brought it up to the baby's lips. The baby drank, his little hands clutching the neck of the bottle. He stopped crying. My dad walked to the other side of the road and beckoned the woman with one finger as though she were a naughty schoolgirl. I thought he was going to reprimand her for feeding the child beer, but then I could see that he spoke to her in that friendly way of his—low voice, hand on shoulder, back turned, walking and nodding. As they parted, he took his cap off and put it on the child's head. The cap must have stank of sweat and wheel grease, but the kid loved it. My dad came back with an orange beaded necklace for me. I shouted, "Beautiful, thank you!" and she took her baby's hand and waved it back at me.

A few hours later, when the sun had set and the truck was fixed, we checked into a hotel as a treat. Beds and linen, hot showers and towels. We even had our own rooms on the second floor. I was about to go to bed when I heard a woman's voice. I poked my head out of the door and looked into the patio downstairs and there she was, the woman with the blue dress, sitting by the pool with my dad. Her skin shone with oil and she wore bracelets, earrings, and necklaces made from the same orange stones as the necklace my dad had given me.

I spied on them. My dad opened two quarts of beer, gave one to her, and put his hand on her thigh. They drank and spoke—in Herero, I think—and she laughed with her whole body, slapping her thighs and throwing her face up to the night sky. I imagined my dad marrying this woman. She would be my stepmother, and she could teach me how to make things, and I had a feeling that she would be kind, and fun. I went to sleep and was woken up in the middle of the night by the sounds of their lovemaking coming from the room next door. Two heavy people boning each other like horny hippos. I wondered if they had waited until they thought I was asleep to do it.

A few days later, on Christmas day, we got to sleep in beds again. My dad's friend Rudolph owned a lodge near Etosha pan. We ate a real meal—lamb and mint sauce, roast potatoes and butternut with brown sugar. Everything, Rudolph said more than once, was "on the house." I had two full plates of the buffet, plus milk tart. The men seemed impressed with how much I ate, for a girl. After supper, my dad and I exchanged Christmas presents. He gave me a kit to light fires with, and a stack of black and white aerial photos he'd had since the war. He must have brought them all the way from Windhoek. I loved them. I gave him a porcupine quill I'd found and a big map I'd drawn that afternoon. It depicted our trip: our little truck following a dotted line tracing our path north, with notable sights colored in with koki pens. There was Festus with his *mielies*, Marco Polo with his bony smile, the pink pom-pom–hatted man, skinny Wimpie and his petrol station, and the woman with the blue dress. The trail ended with a big question mark, and a *To Be Continued . . .*

We hit the bar. It was full of red-faced tourists bragging about their leopard hunts or their black rhino sightings. Rudolph introduced us to a group of diplomats' sons who were on a golfing-safari tour. I fell in love with every one of them, but especially with Johannes, son of the Finnish ambassador to Namibia. He had a long face and delicate hands. I imagined him taking me back to Finland and making me his princess. We would eat herring and listen to punk music together. I thought him superior in every way to Greg, the rugby-playing brute I'd given my virginity away to. I wished then that I had heeded my mother's advice and waited for love.

Johannes handed me a glass of champagne, and then another. I liked the tingle on my tongue, the surge of reckless energy and my racing mind. He took me around the back of the restaurant, put his hands around my waist, and told me I had the most beautiful eyes he'd ever seen. He smelled of pine cones and elephant grass. He kissed me with too much tongue. But still, it was perfect, and I knew suddenly that we would be good together but that we would lose touch and he would go back to his international school and grow up and be handsome and perfect with a more sophisticated woman than I could ever be.

We made a bonfire and someone turned the music up. My dad was still inside, chatting up the bartender. Johannes took my hand and twirled me in circles, faster and faster around the fire. I tried to look gracious and pretty, so the other diplomat's sons would want to dance with me too, but Johannes twirled me back too fast and knocked me in the eye with his elbow.

I fell to the ground.

Johannes said, "Sorry, sorry!" but in a laughing way that made it seem like it was my fault.

Everyone crowded over me. Someone picked me up and walked me back to the lodge. I turned around to see Johannes hunched over, laughing with his friends.

In the kitchen, I was given a pack of frozen peas wrapped in a tea towel. I held it to my bruised eye. Women in white uniforms asked me where my dad was. I felt dizzy and feverish. I was convinced that I had finally contracted malaria and I cursed my dad for skimping on *muti* instead of shelling out for proper medication. (Quinine makes you deaf, he liked to say and did I want to be deaf?) Through the open door, I heard the party reaching fever pitch. It sounded like one long terrifying shriek. I hated them all and longed, for the first time on that trip, for my mother.

The next morning, my dad was sleeping on the bare stone floor of our room. He was wearing a woman's dangly earring in one ear. He reeked of booze. I looked at myself in the mirror. I had a black eye. I decided not to tell my dad about it unless he asked. The noise in the truck made my head thump harder. Behind us, ziggurats of cellophane-wrapped textbooks banged against the metal rods of our tents. Every wire, every screw, every plug, every door panel, every air vent buzzed and rattled. It was like being stuck in a washing machine. The vinyl upholstery oozed crumbs of foam that stuck to my sweaty thighs. The sky was a flat hot white, the clouds thick enough to obscure the sun but thin enough to allow the full assault of milky heat to beat down on our wretched truck. My dad belched and asked me to hand him a jabuli.

I lied and said, "Fresh out."

He still hadn't noticed my bruised eye. I kept my resentment curled up inside me, like a precious imaginary pet.

"What's your problem, kiddo? Bored?"

"Only boring people get bored," I replied, in a sing-song voice, parroting his favorite aphorism.

He snorted. I put my bare feet up on the dashboard, spreading my toes on the muddy windshield.

I put on my adult voice and said, "I just hope we can make up for lost time."

Our detour to visit Rudolph had made us fall behind on the schedule I'd drawn up.

"Patience of a cow, balls of a bull, my girl."

I said, "Can I have a smoke?"

He turned to look at me, too shocked to speak. I didn't really like smoking—I had tried it a few times and it made me nauseous—but I wanted to see if he would say yes. I wanted to see what he was made of.

After a long silence, he said, "Suit yourself," and pulled out a crunched pack of Camels from his shirt pocket. I lit one, inhaled, and resisted the urge to cough. My eyes watered. I blew the smoke out of the open window, imagining myself on a cruise ship headed to Monaco, or driving in a convertible in Hollywood.

We reached Opuwo and stopped at the Standard Bank. I was expecting a routine cash withdrawal, but we were there all afternoon. My dad was trying to get another travel allowance from the Ministry of Education. The manager came out and let my dad use the bank's phone. As my dad boomed into the phone, sweat patches spread under his armpits and across his belly until his khaki shirt was almost sodden. I could tell from the way he was pacing that the bureaucrats on the other side were asking him how he had managed to burn through his last travel allowance in so short a time. I sat on the windowsill watching. I liked to play a game where I imagined that he was completely disconnected from me, so that I could watch his antics with detached bemusement. But the security guard, who had been watching me all afternoon, knew the truth. He stared at me, hard. I fidgeted, looking at my fingers and toes hoping he would stop. Every time I looked up all I saw were the whites of his eyes and the big baton and the smile, as though he was in love with me. I tried to hide behind people in the queue, but by the end of the day as the bank emptied out, there was nowhere left to hide.

At last the Ministry caved in. We got a transfer of cash, enough at least for the last few days' food and diesel. From then on I kept detailed lists of everything we spent money on. Chicken pieces: R45. Beer: R20. Diesel: R216. Gin: R52. Tonic: R14. Ice: R18.

*   *   *

It was getting dark and we were pushing for Epupa Falls. The sky was blue at the top, then pink, dissolving into tiny pockets of molten red behind the mountains. Amoeba-shaped mirrors of water reflected the clouds. At the end of the road, the tar melted into the sky in a shimmering, sugary mess. And I wished it would swallow us up and forget about us.

The next morning, we argued about the best route north. I was in charge of reading the map; he had no patience for such things. He claimed to know the way; I was sure we had made a wrong turn. I suggested turning around to ask for help, instead of wasting diesel and time by pushing on in what was most likely the wrong direction.

"Jeez, Dad," I said. "I'm the one with the map. Just trust me for once."

He didn't answer.

I said, "And maybe if you weren't drunk all the time, you'd actually remember the way."

He slammed on the brakes and we screeched and skidded and then stopped in a cloud of dust. He stared at me with a look I'd never seen before. His eyes were bulging like ping-pong balls. Purple capillaries throbbed around his nose. He looked like he'd just downed a bottle of Witblits.

He said, "Okay—let's go back." His voice was high pitched like a girl's.

I couldn't tell if he was going to strangle me or make me get out of the car and leave me there forever. I said in my smallest possible voice that he was right, I was wrong, we should carry on, and that I was sorry for not trusting him. He didn't answer; he just started up the truck again and pulled back onto the road. I didn't want him to know I was crying, so I stopped breathing and didn't wipe away the tears.

In the end, he was right about the road, but he didn't rub it in.

"Ay-ay-ay-ay-ay, Epupa," he said at last, as we came over the hill tired and bushwhacked.

It was the first thing he'd said since the fight.

"I tell you what, Lizzie, this place, this place . . ." He whistled through his teeth, high and long.

When my dad whistled like that, it meant one thing and one thing only: *drama*. Something major must have gone down here, but he didn't volunteer any details. We stopped and watched the setting sun for a bit. Epupa Falls was the Holy Grail. We were done, finished and *klaar*. Silver-feathered palm trees, the waterfall above and the river burning below. Angola's border was just ahead. An old Himba woman was stooped on the other side, collecting old bullets—left over from the Border War, my dad said. They made jewelry from those bullets and sold them on the side of the road—heavy, glorious pieces that we couldn't afford but that my mother would insist upon having if she were with us.

"Divine, just divine. I'd *die* for those, doll," he said, in the nasty nasal Kugel accent he used for my mother.

I could imagine her trying to barter some of her Woolies blouses for these works of art. She prided herself on deals like that. On a trip to Malawi, she once bartered some of my old t-shirts, a pack of pens, and a calculator for three coffee tables, a wooden chess set, and five intricately woven grass rugs, and we came back to Windhoek with carts piled high like airport Bedouins.

It was different in Epupa. There were no bulky buses farting through the dust, laden with German tourists. There wasn't even a town, just a river and a resort run by Pieter and Ursula, two South African missionaries who had arrived in the seventies. They found no souls worth saving so they opened the Promised Land Lodge and scraped by hosting the few brave or lost travelers who found themselves that far north.

We had been traveling for nearly three weeks. We were covered in dust. My right arm was sunburned and sore to the touch. Our truck spluttered into the driveway then died, miraculously, just as we reached the parking lot. It was some kind of sign, Ursula and Pieter said, and they welcomed us with tea and milk tart. Ursula gave me puzzles to do, called me *bokkie,* and donated some of her daughter's old clothes to me. I felt poor but was grateful. While the men were outside working on the truck, Ursula showed me photos of her children. They had moved away years ago. Her son was a coffee farmer in Zambia, her daughter was working for a PR company in London. I was relieved to have a break from my dad, to see that there were other ways of being in the world. I didn't want his scruffy genes, I wanted to trade mine in for nice new shiny ones, like the ones Ursula's daughter and granddaughter seemed to possess so effortlessly as they stood smiling in front of the Big Ben. I decided to get a perm and shave my legs when I got home, two things I'd promised my dad I would never do.

It would take four days for the spare parts we needed to arrive from Windhoek. I washed blood and soggy lettuce leaves off the few remaining beers and hid them in my backpack. I drank them down by the river, listening to the tinkling music it made. I stared across the water into Angola's jungle as though it contained some kind of hidden code.

All night long, the adults talked about how Namibia was going downhill and how much better it was in the good-old-bad-days when it was South West. Pieter had fought in the Border War too, as a Parabat—part of the parachute battalion, back in the days when South Africa still had a draft. My dad and Pieter stayed up late swapping stories and comparing shrapnel scars. Pieter shed his gentle Christian veneer and acted out daring battle scenes where the Angolans always retreated like cowards and never cleaned their weapons. Pieter said the Cuban general had an axe to grind with Namibia because when the war was over, all the general got for his heroic efforts was an electric fan. A lousy fan! My dad and Pieter laughed about that fan for a long time.

Pieter had told my dad we could stay for free while we were waiting for the truck parts, but by the third day at the Promised Land Lodge, our hosts stiffened toward us. The G&Ts were no longer on the house. Ursula put me to work making beds in the guest rooms. She taught me how to do hospital corners and how to use the computer to make reservations when people called. Hardly anyone ever did, but she still made sure there was a fresh daisy in a glass in every room, every day.

Despite Ursula's stoniness, I was glad to be there, and Christina, the cleaning girl, was nice to me. She did my makeup, gently stroking a ridiculous amount of blue eye shadow onto my closed eyelids. She told me she was going to marry Michael, the cook, as soon as she turned eighteen. They planned to go to Johannesburg together to look for good jobs. I wanted to go with them. I told her I could be their nanny; I could look after their babies while they worked. She threw her head back and belly laughed.

"You are so silly, Lizzie!"

I was serious. I didn't want to go back to Windhoek, back to Gary's house with its shiny tiled floors and lavender walls. I didn't want to go back to my dad's house either, to the piles of rotting wood and rows of empty gin bottles.

Christina said she could fix my sunburned arm. We walked to a Himba village just beyond the lodge grounds. A few women sat beneath a canopy with children playing around them. One woman was sewing beads onto a cloth of bright blue. Another was grinding something on a stone. There was a plangence to their chatter, to the scraping. There were no men around. The women greeted Christina with bemused respect; I could tell they liked her. We sat for a while under the canopy while Christina spoke with them and I played with the babies.

Christina led me by the pinky finger to a hut. Inside, an old woman was seated cross-legged. Ash was swirling around her in slow motion. She had a wide gap between her front teeth. Christina told her about my arm and left us alone.

The woman poured a butterfat-ochre mixture out of a tin onto a stone. She mixed it around with a spoon, then tested it on the crook of her arm. She smiled at me as she slathered my arms with the mixture. It smelled like resin, like moon-rocks mixed with juniper berries. We exchanged no words. I wanted more than anything to ask her if she knew of a young boy around my age whose mother called him Jono.

I had nothing with which to repay her kindness. I left and said, "*Dankie, baie, baie dankie*" and vowed to return with a gift.

But the next day, we left the resort without the truck parts, and without the truck. My dad shook my shoulders to wake me up and said, "We're leaving, *geddup*."

Pieter and Ursula's driver was waiting outside our rondavel with his engine idling. We threw our bags in the back of the *bakkie*. Standing by the gate was Christina, about to start her morning rounds with a bucket in one hand and a mop in the other. I lifted my hand up to wave but saw that her face was ashen and her eyes puffy, like she'd been crying all night. She looked at me with the look of lead, the look that fills everything up. I wanted to cry out to her, *Peri Nawa? Christina, are you well?* I looked at my dad. He was passed out, snoring already. His blond-gray curls were bouncing, hatefully cherubic. I said, almost to myself, "Daddy." It was the last time I called him that.

We drove to the airstrip in silence. Geel dropped us off and chucked our bags on the pavement. My dad hobbled to the office and as I picked up my rucksack, Geel said to me, "Yussus, your dad's a *poes*. I feel sorry for your mother."

It hurt for a second and then suddenly I didn't care about what my dad had done to make us have to leave so soon. I didn't care about my mother or floppy Brandon. I just cared about myself. I gave Geel my fakest fake smile.

Inside the tiny airport office my dad was trying to cadge a deal, promising discounts on his tours for their clients if they gave us a good price on a flight back to Windhoek. We loaded our bags onto a tiny plane. The propellers thrummed and the cabin shuddered. It was my first time in such a small plane and I hated being able to see the controls, how much petrol was left, the overweight pilot sleepily pressing buttons above his head. A dog chased our plane all the way down the airstrip until we took off. From the sky, Epupa Falls was a lick of deep green on kilometers of beige. The road below that we'd driven on for days, now cut the dry earth like an X-Acto blade on paper. Straight black lines elbowed left, right, left and right, until we were home.

A week later, my dad flew back up to Epupa Falls with the parts he needed, fixed the truck himself, and drove all the way back to Windhoek alone.

*   *   *

Before my dad died, I took my husband home to meet him. When we got to Windhoek in the middle of the night after a transcontinental flight, we found him in the driveway in khaki shorts, no shirt, with the distended belly of a pregnant woman, drinking a G&T (a triple, if I know my dad), smoking and fixing the gearbox of a friend's Land Rover.

The pain was driving him crazy. During the day, he would take off all his clothes and walk around in the garden, arms outstretched like Jesus on the cross, smiling, with his face to the sun. That's how I think of him now. And I think of him driving along a long stretch of empty road, holding the steering wheel tight.

And I think of a Himba boy who is now a man my age, living somewhere in Northern Namibia or out in the wide, wide, world, whose mother calls him Jono.

DARA KELL *is an award-winning writer and documentary filmmaker. Her films have been broadcast on PBS, TVFrance, and Netflix, and screened at festivals worldwide. Dara has made films in Brazil, Azerbaijan, Egypt, and China, and is currently making a documentary about Reverend William Barber and civil disobedience in America. Her short story "Small Holding" won the* Zoetrope: All-Story *Fiction Contest in 2015. Dara is a graduate of Rhodes University and lives in Brooklyn and Cape Town.*

————————

The God in the Dark

Leeyee Lim

After the semester closes in the spring, after I have tired of the incessant complaining rains, I take a train that moves west from the middle of the country to the coast. I have chosen to do this in the spring because I know that when summer comes with its extended sunlight pushing at me and stretching my nerves to fraying point, I will have little energy left for a trip of this sort. In summer, something akin to rage rises inside me, a fist shaking itself at the relentless sunlight.

The straight lines of the highway are a relief to the eye as I drive to the train station in the next city. On either side are the cornfields, flat and wide and already green, familiar to me, even though a year ago I had never before seen an ear of corn growing on its stalk. I leave my car in the covered parking lot, the underground air still chilly despite the season. The main hall of the station is a soaring marble monstrosity, the ceiling carved with cherubs, the wooden benches clustered in the center dwarfed by the giant pillars supporting the roof. In the waiting lounge, there is a large group of young people—fifteen or twenty of them—sitting amidst their duffle bags and backpacks. They talk loudly, tapping at laptops and phones, the girls eating carrot sticks out of a Ziploc bag. One boy naps with his head thrown back over his seat, spindly legs sprawling halfway across the aisle. They look as though they've been camped out here for days, as if they are intending to make the station their permanent home. I think of my own students.

Smoke billows from the silvery train as I walk down the platform, engulfing a uniformed attendant as he pushes a cart. Soon, I am standing in my berth, pleasantly surprised by its size and relative luxury. I have dipped into my savings and splurged on a single sleeper with a private bathroom. I don't mind the expense. I have always been shy about sharing intimate spaces. The handful of lovers I have had were never welcome to stay the night. I cannot abide the idea of another body sleeping through the night beside me, their breath warm and humid and moist. I cannot imagine myself waking up to another person—to shared morning smells and bathroom sounds. Not for me the cozy side-by-side toothbrushing, no.

I hang my jacket on the coat hook and set my bag down on the hard, blue carpet. There is a long couch on one end, which I assume folds out into a bed, as there are two snowy white pillows sitting on it. There is a floor-length mirror, a small sink with a trash can underneath, and a closet-sized washroom with a shower attachment. A notice fixed to the wall advises me to shower while seated on the closed toilet lid.

There is a knock on the door of the berth and I open it to find a train attendant standing there. His uniform is gray and his name tag is trimmed in red and red curlicues announces his name: Gary. He clutches a clipboard against his ample stomach and smiles.

"Good afternoon, ma'am," he says. "My name is Gary and I'm going to be your attendant for the journey." He glances surreptitiously behind me but makes no comment about my being alone.

I remain silent and he looks down at his clipboard. "So you're going to—let me see—San Francisco. Is that right?"

"Yes, that's right."

"All the way, huh? End of the line." I am silent.

"Well, you're in for a real treat. It's a beautiful journey, full of sights."

Again, I am silent. I am not a taciturn person by nature but I resent having to respond to meaningless comments.

Gary blinks a little then looks down at his clipboard again. "Okay, then, ma'am, what time would you like to have dinner?" I have read about this. I did my research before buying my ticket. Train passengers pick a time slot and then proceed to the restaurant car when their dinner service is announced.

"What time do most people usually have dinner?"

Gary makes a little thinking frown. "I'd say seven, seven thirty-ish?"

"And what's the earliest dinner slot?"

"Five thirty, ma'am. But that's early for most."

"I'll have it at five thirty, then."

"Five thirty it is." He makes a note on his clipboard and hands me a small white card with my dinner time on it. He turns to go just as I remember something else I read online.

"Gary?" I say. He turns back around, looks at me enquiringly. "Private sleeper passengers have the option of having dinner served in their compartment, is that right?"

"Yes, ma'am. Would you like to do that instead?"

I hesitate. "No," I say. "But can you arrange for that tomorrow night?"

"Certainly," he says. He closes the door behind him.

I sit by the window and draw one of the pillows to me, placing it behind my head. I lean back and close my eyes and don't open them again until I feel and hear the train begin to pull out of the station.

* * *

Back at the university, I taught an introductory course on world mythology. Z was a junior who showed up for class on the first day wearing an Overwatch sweatshirt—I recognized the logo because my office-mate played the game—and khaki shorts that were fraying at the seams, tendrils of thread hanging down his bare legs. The skin on his knees was red and chapped. He had the kind of straight, floppy hair that always put me in mind of the rabbits that overran the town in summer.

An adjunct professor's job is underpaid and often miserable. Academia is not for the faint of heart. And yet, I could not help but like my job. I liked the way it shaped my week, the rhythm of the seven days—named after the Norse gods, of course—dictated by the days I taught, the days I held office hours and graded papers. Teaching gave my life a sense of order and I am the sort of person who has always prized order.

In fact, it's what first drew me to mythology as a child. On the surface, the Greek and Roman myths, the Egyptian and Norse tales of creation and destruction, appear to be a confused tangle of relationships, of twisting family trees and incest—why, my students invariably wanted to know, did they all have to marry their siblings? Were there not enough attractive gods to go around?—but I saw beyond that to the truth: mythology was, above all, an organizational system. It was a way to make of the raw chaos of the universe an order of some kind. It was endlessly fascinating to me.

Yes, on the whole I liked teaching. And there was also this: my students, against all odds, interested me. Many of them were avid video game players, as I soon discovered. They pointed out to me the close parallels between video games and mythology—not just the games that were actually based on the classical myths but also the fact that video games so often dealt with the same themes: the interplay between good and evil, free will and fate. I had no interest in video games, but their expertise in their chosen field impressed me. It took commitment and obsession—two things I admire—to become as well-versed in the gaming world as they were. I have never had any patience for amateurs and hobbyists.

The fact that I liked my students surprised me. I had never wanted children—an act of self-aggrandizement if I ever saw one—and I could not imagine myself as a mother. Unlike most women my age, I have always been indifferent to babies.

But interacting with my students week after week, I began to see how a mother's heart might break at the sight of the first down on a boyish lip, the husky deepening of a once-childish voice, the touchingly curly and sparse hairs on a leg. When he leaned in to speak to me in class, Z had the brightest and starriest eyes I had ever seen on a real-life boy.

* * *

The train is still moving slowly through the outskirts of the city when I open my eyes. There is the murmur of the engines, the muffled sound of people moving around in the passageway outside my compartment. I ease my shoes off and lie back down, stretching out on the couch.

I have always taken a strange pleasure in being alone while surrounded by strangers. Airplane bathrooms in the middle of long-haul flights, turning the lock as people all around snooze in the dark cabin. At the cinema, when the lights dim and you can no longer see your neighbors but can still hear the rustle of hands reaching into popcorn bags. I have even felt it on the rare occasions I go to the mall, the wearying rigmarole of taking clothes off and putting them on again and asking for a different size leavened only by the cozy pleasure of hearing other women in the changing rooms doing the same. Often, I wonder if I am the only person who feels this way.

* * *

Two weeks into the semester, Z came to my office hours. He lingered by the door after knocking, wearing his customary threadbare shorts and cork sandals—this, despite the snow on the ground—his backpack slung casually over one shoulder. There was something studied in that casualness.

"Professor? Can I come in?"

I had told my students to address me by name—I have never felt comfortable with the title of professor, although I imagine that one day I will be. But Z persisted, always pronouncing the title with a certain stiff, old-fashioned formality and yet with a twinkle in his eye that hinted at some private joke I was supposed to share with him. I nodded. "Sure."

I felt a little thrill as he sat down. My office, which I shared with another colleague, was really nothing more than a glorified cubicle with some bookshelves. Up close, I could see the freckles on his nose, the way his eyelashes curled upward. I noticed that his eyes were actually a dark brown instead of the black I had thought them to be.

Most students who come to my office hours are looking to bargain for a higher grade or plead an unexcused absence. So I was unprepared for it when Z slid his backpack from his shoulder to the ground and leaned forward in his seat and said, "Professor, do you believe in god?"

I stared at him. At first, I thought he was joking, but his face was perfectly serious. I considered the question. Any discussion, I have always felt, must begin with a definition of the terms discussed.

"What do you mean by that term?"

"Well, you teach us about mythology, which is all about gods. So I was just wondering if you yourself believe in god."

I was puzzled, but I answered with certainty. "If you're asking me if I believe in the gods we talk about in class—Odin, Thor, Zeus—then no, I do not."

Z seemed disappointed by my reply, as if the question had been a test I had not known I was sitting for, one I had clearly failed. "So you don't really believe in any of it?"

"Not in a literal sense, no."

He nodded thoughtfully but seemed unconvinced. I began to grow impatient. What was it the boy wanted from me? Just for good measure, I added, "I don't believe in the god of the Abrahamic religions either."

At this, Z waved a hand dismissively, as if the faith of over half of the world's population was a nonissue. He sat back in his chair. "So basically you don't believe in anything?"

I shrugged a little at this. The response seemed at odds with Z's usual manner. *You don't believe in anything*—it was the accusation of a child unwilling to believe that the world could be so cruel as to offer one nothing to believe in.

"Why are you asking me this?"

"I suppose I'm curious."

"And you?"

I am pretty sure, in this day and age of political correctness, that one is not supposed to ask a student about their religious beliefs. Z raised an eyebrow. "I was raised in a Catholic household," he said. Then he stood up and stretched, his shirt lifting a little so that I caught a glimpse of smooth skin, tiny whorls of hair that disappeared down the waist band of his pants. I averted my eyes. He reached for his backpack. "Thanks for your time, Professor. See you around."

As he walked out the door, he paused before a small figurine sitting on my bookcase. It was a plaster cast in the classical style, a woman with her arm raised as if frozen in the act of lifting an invisible curtain.

Z picked it up and held it to the light, turning back to me. "Psyche, right?"

I nodded, surprised and rather impressed. There could not have been many undergrads who could identify the figurine so easily. Most people knew instead of Cupid, Psyche's lover, he of the bow and arrow, nowadays infantilized and so crassly associated with Valentine's Day. Z turned it over in his hand, a smile playing on his lips as if he was thinking of something pleasant. "She wanted to look upon his face," he murmured.

I was surprised yet again. "Yes," I said.

He put the figurine back on the shelf and turned to me, his silhouette outlined by the lamp light in the hall. "And if you were the beloved of an ancient god, Professor, wouldn't you want to look upon his face?"

"I—"

But he was gone, the door closed behind him. I sat at my desk for a few moments and then walked to the bookcase and picked up the little Psyche. Was it my imagination or was it still warm from his hands? The story of Psyche was not exactly a myth but it fell along similar lines. She was a mortal woman with whom Cupid had fallen in love. Cupid's mother, Venus, had forbidden him from showing Psyche his face and so he took to visiting her at night. The two were happy for a while until Psyche's sisters, jealous of her happiness, goaded her into lighting a lamp one night to look at Cupid's face—thus disobeying Venus and earning Psyche her punishment.

It was not one of my favorite tales. I had always thought Psyche an insipid woman, weak of character, to be so easily persuaded by her sisters. But then again, as Z had said, wouldn't I have wanted to see the god's face?

I thought of the last lover I'd had, a fellow adjunct from another department. We had met at a bar one night, when I had stopped in for a drink and my office-mate had stood up from a crowded table in the corner and waved me over. Everyone had been from the university—it was that sort of town. He was slight, with sloping shoulders, and as I looked at his fingers as he gesticulated to emphasize a point, I sipped my beer and thought, *maybe*.

Later that night, I made it clear that he was not welcome to stay and he left. We never spoke to each other again. So perhaps not. Perhaps I was the sort of person who was content to take the pleasure and leave the rest in the dark.

Z never did come to my office again. But the strangeness of the encounter stayed with me, as did the jolt of nameless emotion I felt every time my eye fell on the Psyche figurine in my office. As the semester continued I became gradually aware that it was his face I looked forward to seeing each week in class, the way it looked when he was interested in a point of discussion, the way he leaned forward in his seat, those long lashes encircling those bright eyes. His questions in class were thoughtful, his willingness to challenge me exciting rather than exasperating, and if he had a tendency to dominate the discussion at times, I was aware that I turned the other cheek for the sheer pleasure of hearing his voice.

* * *

Dusk is already falling by the time I leave my compartment and make my way to the dining car, steadying myself as the train sways on its tracks. It's not as empty as I had hoped. There are a few seated passengers already, and to my surprise, I recognize some of them as part of the group of students I had seen in the waiting lounge back at the station. At one table, the servers are piling cutlery and paper napkins into small baskets. One of them sees me standing by the door and gets up, coming towards me with a basket and a menu.

"How many?"

"One, please."

"Right. Just so you know, ma'am, it's our policy to group diners who aren't already in a party of four. It's to maximize seating, you understand."

I nod. This, too, I already know from my research and I have come prepared with a book. But to my dismay, I am seated with two of the girls from the student group, their group having split into several tables. The girls look up and smile as I slide gingerly into the narrow seat.

I order a salad and grilled fish, with rice pudding for dessert and white wine. It seems to be a safe enough order. The wine comes in a clear plastic cup and is so astringent that I wince at the first sip. There is nothing to see now outside the windows, just shapes in the darkness.

The girls ask me where I am going, what I do back home, do I like the Midwest. I clutch my book in my lap and reply: San Francisco, adjunct professor, yes. Their manner changes a little when I tell them what I do for a living. They ask me what I teach and I say mythology.

"Oh, you mean like Thor and all?" one of the girls asks. Her brown hair is done up in a long braid that hangs over her shoulder, the feathery end almost dipping into the ketchup on her plate.

I'm briefly annoyed. There have recently been a string of atrocious films featuring an overmuscled actor as Thor and no doubt this is the only version of Thor the girl knows. I have seen one of these films, I have to confess. "Yes, like Thor."

The other girl is about to say something else when mercifully, their group decides to leave en masse. My two tablemates say goodbye and then I am alone. I take out my book, find my page, and settle in.

I am reading a retelling of the Perseus myth, aimed at younger readers. It is not, it has to be understood, the kind of book I usually read. But one of my students had mentioned it in class and I had picked it up out of curiosity.

"Hey, my son is reading that," says the server, setting down my plate. "Do you like it?"

"I'm enjoying it very much, thank you," I say.

He looks at me for a moment and then nods. "Right, let me know if you need anything else."

By the time I finish my dinner, the dining car is crowded and noisy. I make my way back to my compartment, finding relief in the quiet that greets me when I shut the door. All that semester long, as my thoughts became more and more entwined with Z, I had listened to the trains passing through our university town. From the wide windows of my apartment, I could see the tracks and at night, I watched the moving lights and lit windows of the passenger trains as they moved through the frigid air. Sometimes, I would wake in the dark and hear the melancholy whistle of one as it passed me by, going somewhere else.

They seemed to be a portent of sorts, these trains, although of what I did not know. I only knew that after so many months of watching, it was a relief to finally be on one, bisecting the night and moving across the country.

That night, when I turn off the lights and unfold my train-issued blanket, the air is so dry that static electricity sparks within the fabric. I was unaware that static electricity was visible to the naked eye but there it is, green sparkles that jump in and out of the thin wool. Unnerved, I bundle the blanket away in a corner of the luggage rack and shiver underneath the thin sheets until the gentle rocking of the train lulls me to sleep.

*　*　*

There was a day near the end of the semester when, coming out of another class I was teaching, I saw Z standing outside the building, a bicycle lock in his hands. He turned and saw me and smiled.

"Hello, Professor," he said. He held up the lock. "I guess someone stole my bike."

I readjusted my grip on my tote bag, brimming with assignment sheets and papers. He could have taken the bus. Or gotten a ride from a classmate. I made a decision. "Where do you live?"

All the way across the parking lot to my car, I was aware of his presence beside me, his stride long and loping, his hair a little longer than when I had first met him, curling around the bottom edge where it clung to his neck. As I opened the car door, Z slid into the passenger seat. In the confined space, in the dimly lit parking ramp, he seemed to have grown bigger somehow. I had noticed this about Z—that he had a tendency to project, at times, an aura of self-assurance that was uncommon in my other students.

There were other things that set him apart. He did not indulge in small talk during those empty minutes before class began. He did not ever use the five-minute break I gave them to check his phone as so many of the others did. I realized, suddenly, that I had never seen him on a bicycle. In our college town, I often saw my other students whizzing around on the bike paths. If they saw me they would wave and grin and say something like "See you next week." It used to give me a strange feeling of dissonance, like when I went to a coffee shop and discovered a student of mine behind the counter. It disquieted me, this bleeding of my professional life into the personal.

And yet here Z was, in my car. He was silent as we drove through the empty streets downtown. I was reminded of the time he had come to my office hours and asked me about god. In my mind's eye, I could see him standing by the door, holding the little figurine of Psyche. The light from the hallway had shone on his hair and forehead and it had struck me then, how much he resembled—in spirit, if not in actual physicality—the ancient Greek sculptures of young men. Kouroi, they were called. Man and boy and god all at once.

"Psyche was right, you know," Z said, breaking the silence, as if he knew what I had been thinking about.

My heart beat a little faster. I shifted in my seat and made a left turn. We were almost there. Z had said that he shared a house with two friends near the edge of town.

"If you're sleeping with a god, you really have the right to know."

I was silent. It was only now that I noticed there was a layer of dust coating my dashboard. How had I missed it? The rest of the car was spotless.

"Don't you agree?" Z persisted.

"Psyche was a foolish woman," I said finally. "She paid the price for it."

"But she had her happy ending, didn't she?"

"Not until she had survived her punishment."

"She thought it was worth it."

The certainty with which he said it puzzled me. The truth was that I thought little of Psyche. She had earned her punishment, I always thought. And worse, in the story she is set a number of challenges to complete before being allowed to reunite with Cupid and she fails to actually do any of them. At every turn she was saved by some outside force—helpful ants, magical reeds. Psyche was the original damsel in distress.

"Why do you have a statue of her in your office if you think she's so foolish?" Z asked.

I had pulled up outside his house, a two-story Queen Anne cottage with a crumbling front porch. "It was a gift," I said, unwilling to admit the truth—that I had bought it in a strip mall gift store, thinking that it was the sort of thing a teacher of mythology should have in her office.

In the fading light, Z's eyes and face were very bright, almost supernaturally so, and as he turned to me I felt my heart contract. This was the enigma of Z, the coin that I flipped over and over in my head as he sat across from me in class. Boy. Man. Boy. Man. Boy. If there was a third side to the coin and I did not see it then, who can blame me now?

He leaned in close and for a moment I thought he would kiss me. But he only stared into my face, frowning ever so slightly. Then he turned away and picked up his backpack and opened the car door. Cool air gushed in and I felt a chill that had nothing to do with the cold. I wanted to hold out my hand, to stay his leaving somehow, to touch him. But just like that time in my office, he was already gone.

I sat in my car for a minute. It was full dark by now and the street was shadowy. I felt bereft. After a moment, I put the car in gear and started the drive home.

It was always on nights like these when, driving back to my apartment, the day's teaching done, that my life seemed the most real to me, as if the darkness falling and the solidity of the steering wheel underneath my fingers gave my life its only semblance of reality. I would be gripped by a familiar fear: that when I left this place—and I always left—my life here would vanish. That, like all the places I have left behind, this one, too, would take on the unreality of a dream that dissipated in the morning light.

A few weeks after that, the Psyche figurine disappeared from my office. I asked my colleague about it but she only shrugged and said she hadn't noticed it there in the first place.

*   *   *

It happens at breakfast the next morning. The train has crossed into Colorado and when the train stopped to refuel at Denver, the air had been high and thin and clear when I stepped out for a short walk.

I have just seated myself for breakfast and found my place in my book when I sense someone standing by my table.

"What are you reading, Professor?"

I look up and Z is standing next to my table, threadbare shorts, backpack and all. I feel myself go very still and then, from deep inside, an upwelling of cold excitement. He sits down in the booth opposite me and grins. I cannot breathe.

"What are you doing here?"

The words come out as a whisper and I am instantly ashamed of how melodramatic they sound, how much they give away.

"I like trains," he says, as if this was a perfectly reasonable explanation. He reaches into his backpack and pulls out something small and crumpled. He smooths it gently, the gesture somehow touching, before handing it to me.

It's a postcard-size reproduction of a painting, the kind you can buy at any museum gift store. A shadowy room, a man and a woman, a chaise. I recognize the eagle in the corner, the red cloak, the brightness around the man's head, the dying throes: the death of Semele.

"To replace your Psyche," Z says. I look up at him. It suddenly strikes me that he is different, somehow. There are subtle changes but they are there. The slightest suggestion of crow's feet, the faintest shadow of a beard, a knowing look in those eyes. I blink and his face is that of a much older man, full bearded, eyes serious. It had been a bright day but now the train car darkens with thunder and lightning and far away I hear the cry of an eagle. I catch my breath. What is this?

I blink again and everything goes back to normal. But I know what I saw and it sends a heat coursing right through me. Z is gone, in his place an elderly gentleman in a bucket hat, sliding gingerly into the booth across from me. The server takes the man's order and I stare, unseeing, as all around me my fellow passengers eat and and talk.

I look down at the postcard in my hand, turning it over and over. Semele, mother of twice-born Dionysus, lover of Zeus. Another woman who wished to look upon his divinity, to know that what was felt in the dark was real. My mind searches for explanations. Perhaps he really is traveling to California. Perhaps that is where he is from. He might even be with the group of students I saw earlier.

Or perhaps it was a trick of the light after all. The thin air of Denver. A conjuring.

But I am grasping for a multitude of possibilities in order to deny the thing I most want to believe: he is here because of me.

*   *   *

All that long day I look for his face in vain. I spend hours in the observation car as the train snakes slowly through the Colorado canyons. My thoughts circle each other and the day passes slowly until, exhausted, I give up and retire to my room.

Gary appears with my dinner tray and sets the tiny table next to my window. I have ordered steak and a baked potato, watery vegetables. I eat it all, slowly, staring out my window and seeing nothing until, as we pull into our stop somewhere in Utah, I see a father and his small son kneeling by the train tracks. There is the barest touch of day left in the sky and they are both wearing identical baseball jerseys, the boy's so large it engulfs him almost completely. Their faces are beaming, haloed in the fiery light, as the father points out the train to his son and tells him to wave. I keep watching, unable to take my eyes off them, but in a matter of moments the sun sinks completely and their faces become ghostly smudges in the darkness.

I think about my apartment and the sound of a train whistle in the night. My tiny office, piled high with dusty papers. The young faces of my students, turned to me in curiosity, in enthusiasm, in boredom. I have the strangest feeling that I will never see any of it again, that like the pioneers who had moved west following this very route, I will leave everything behind and make a new start.

The night is chilly and I reach for the blanket I had bundled into a corner yesterday. I am no longer afraid as I spread it over myself, green sparks moving through the fabric like fireflies, like the brightness in a boy's eye as he leans in to speak to me. I find the postcard of Semele and prop it on the sink beside the bed.

I lie down and close my eyes and listen to the hum of the engines, allow my body to be rocked by the train as it moves through the night across this country, from settlement to settlement amidst the wilderness. From light to light. The air is thin and cold. I think of the train's route on the map of this country like a constellation. I think of Semele and Psyche and all the other women who have loved a god in the dark. I am not afraid. A heavy scent of oak and olives fills the room and I wonder: what is it that they want from us? What is it that they have always wanted? I have no answers. But I know that if I wait long enough, travel far enough, the god will reveal itself to me and I will surrender.

LEEYEE LIM *is a Malaysian-Chinese writer who currently lives and writes in Toronto. Her fiction has previously been published or is forthcoming in* Epiphany Magazine, The Drum Literary Magazine *and* Necessary Fiction. *She taught creative writing at the University of Iowa and is a graduate of the Iowa Writers' Workshop*

Pirating

Jack Foraker

"These waters are cursed," Fa told us on the drive to Trinidad. Choked on trash and shipwrecks. Fed by melted icebergs and moony currents. Coves teeming with creepy-crawlies, fluoride, and mercury, "maybe even treasure," as our Fa said, if only we knew where to dig. Old salt bearing north in his janked sedan, us unseatbelted in back and whining all the way. The legroom was littered with clamshells, crumpled wrappers, and gas-station receipts, the air dank from fast food and manhood. When finally Fa gave the ahoy, parking in front of a clapboard rental, we tumbled gasping into the grass, stretched our limbs to quaking as though we'd been months without solid ground. But Fa, no fan of our dramatics, kicked at our ribs with his black boots, gentle-like— "Get up." Captain to our crew. "Act precious and we're going straight home." Then he walked up to the front door, leaving us to follow.

We were staying in a beat rental on a bluff thing, north of Trinidad proper. The roof was splapped in seagull poop, ice plants teething at the foundation. It was close enough to the cove that waves would leap and hit the windows if the waters were rough enough, which they always were. Fa took the rental's only bed, so we got stuck with a futon in the living room. During the nights, we slept backs to each other and tug-of-warred for the dinky blanket. But during the days, Fa let us do basically anything. We chugged sports drinks the color of glaciers and macaws, built driftwood forts just to wreck them when we got bored. Our noses sniffled red with cold—much as Fa's own with too much grog—but we didn't care because he didn't care. There were no rules in Trinidad, no Mom to suck the fun out of everything. If we played videos too loud on his tablet or tracked sand inside, he wouldn't make us stop or even say anything. "Dude Trip," Fa kept saying. Just he and we.

* * *

This was the last summer I pretended Seb and I were twins. We had the same eyes, the same hair color and height, the same parents, but all we were was brothers. It was easy to tell us apart. Sometimes people thought I was older, but it was Seb who had hair brambling his pits, a treasure trail from belly button to crotch, one long dark tendril curling out his neck. A sabre-cut ran down my brother's chest, and in Trinidad, he flaunted this scar like something battle earned, instead of something from heart surgery. He was always shirtless on Dude Trip, always in his swim trunks, always asking when we'd go down to the cove, always jonesing to explore. Seb was eleven. I was nine.

When Fa finally did take us down that first day, he said to stay in the shallows. The cove was a pulverized hook of beach, gloomy and gray. Ghost ships of fog crashed against rocks jutting out from the deeps, which Fa called *sea stacks*. This prompted a lecture on wave erosion, coastal geography, how anything could be out there: Russian shipwrecks from the fur-trading days, when there were so many otters you could kill them just for fun; fish with straw-clogged gills; "Mermaids, maybe?" Fa said. His lips twitched as if he already knew the answer.

Seb bolted for the water. People stared because he was screaming his head off and—I hate that I thought this—maybe also because he has Down syndrome. Fa looked at me with some annoyance as Seb hurled himself into the ocean.

"Go get him."

And I did. I loved when Fa signaled how I was the real first mate.

I followed Seb into the water. The waves shoved themselves at me, but I didn't fall. I knew that, between me and my brother, I was the better swimmer.

"You have to get out."

Seb ignored me and tried to float. "Man," he said. "This is the life."

"Fa told me to get you." I went and pulled at his arm. "Come on."

"No. Just come on this way, instead." And he pulled back harder. He pulled us under.

* * *

We came out soaking, teeth crab-clacking. Fa wrapped a towel around us to share and said to be more careful. "Those waves will fuck you if you aren't."

We shivered and clutched the towel against ourselves. A lady walked by with her hands stuffed in the pockets of her sweats. Her baseball hat in Humboldt State green, her sunglasses like two lightless pits. She said hi, and we said hi back. She asked if we liked the beach, and even though I couldn't see her eyes, I knew which part of *we* she was looking at.

She squatted at Seb's level and said, "You having fun, bud?"

"It's awesome," he said. She smiled, friendly faced, but I could tell she hadn't understood what he said. She reached out and tousled his hair. Fa clenched his fists till the knuckles popped.

"So lucky—at the beach with your dad and bro. You seen the tide pools? They're *awesome*."

"We're heading there, thanks," Fa said. He told her to have a nice day, and once she was gone, he told us, "Fuck her," cutting his tongue on the curse. A dagger twixt his goldish teeth. He ran a hand through his hair—longer than ours, matted round his pale face. His arms were jungled with tattoos, tribal jags and cursive prayers. He had rings on every finger, gifts he'd given Mom back when they didn't hate each other. Once they started to, he took them all back. As the lady left, he worried those gems and pearls and said, "Okay, crew. Let's check out those tide pools."

The rocks were sharp under our bare feet, but Fa helped us both along. He told us to poke anemones and watch them recoil from our touch. He brushed his fingers on an urchin's spines and the rest aimed at his hand, sensing danger. I wondered if creatures that brainless even worried about dying.

"Careful of this guy," he said. "Wouldn't want to step on him."

But Fa was the one wearing boots, and with one good stomp, he broke it, dug through the cracked shell, spines still twitching on the dregs of life, and pulled loose something like a wedge of citrus. Slick and bright orange. He rinsed it with saltwater, then popped the whole organ into his mouth, making a show of it.

"Gonads," he said. "Wanna try?" There were more of them within the urchin's broken body. We looked at each other, each waiting for the other to be first.

*   *   *

No one told us about the urchins. How they were marauding the coastline, killing the kelp and the coral. No one told us how the abalones were now so shriveled and inbred they couldn't even grip the rocks right, or how the starfish were ripping off their own limbs for no apparent reason. No one told us about the blob of warm water that had drifted up from the Southern Hemisphere, those tropical waters full of tropical thingamabobs. By the summer of Dude Trip, Trinidad's shallows were thick with oil and plastic, purple snails from Mexico and spindly crabs from Japan, seaweed and scrap metal—litter, really, and we mistook it all for loot.

The next afternoon, Fa let us go alone to the tide pools while he watched news on his tablet, headphones stuffed so deep into the nautili of his ears that he couldn't hear us at all. Mom wouldn't have done that. She would have watched us close, seen us wandering farther than we should. But she was back in Sacramento, three hundred miles south.

The tide pools were more crowded than before, and warmer. The worst of the clouds had burned away, leaving just the sherbet melt of sundown. We didn't talk to anyone besides each other. Seb combed through the puddles and over the rocks—scheming, I knew, looking for something worth taking. He eased into a deep pool, and I didn't say anything when he dove down. We weren't supposed to swim alone, Seb especially. I looked back at Fa but could only make out the smudge of him. Seen afar, he looked less like a captain and more like someone who wore skinny jeans to a beach. Seb bubbled up, holding something.

"Jackpot," he said.

What he found was a tarnished lockbox, small but crazy heavy. And not even locked. Inside were doubloons, hundreds of them, silver and gold. We dug our fingers through them, and I got so drunk off the thought of finding actual treasure that I didn't think to ask the real question until later. Not who this all belonged to, or how it had gotten here, but this: how had Seb noticed that dull box, among all the cove's brighter colors?

* * *

"Treasure?" Fa said, when we booked it back to show him. "You mean coins."

Only then did we realize: copper, not gold. Quarters, not doubloons. Seb examined a penny curdled with verdigris and frowned. "This is definitely not a penny."

"Put it on your tongue, bud." Fa took one and held it in his mouth. "Feel how it warms up? Real gold stays cold. You found spare change."

"Whatever. Nobody cares." Seb joked to hide his letdown. "I never thought it was really real."

We waited for Fa to make us put it all back, return it to the sea like some shell or coral, but he kept staring at the lockbox. Then he raised his eyebrows, scheming himself.

"I mean, it *is* a lot," he said. "How much do you think we've got here? Like in dollars?"

* * *

Due south, in Eureka, Fa said there was a machine that turned coins into dollars. So that night we piled into his car, lockbox between us as Fa sped down 101, slowing only when we hit rain. Not a lot: fifteen seconds of storm, smooth sailing after that. But you could tell from the asphalt's shimmer in the almost-empty parking lot we pulled into that the rain had rolled through just before us. Fa's boots splashed the puddles as he led us into the gargantuan box of a store. We were both barefoot.

Inside was stagnant cold and flecked linoleum, bleached wash of light down the rows of panini presses, fishing poles, star-spangled crud. It was almost July. The machine Fa spoke of was at the front of the store, a green rectangle between a DVD rental kiosk and a key duplicator—Coinstar. "Knew they'd have one," he said, taking the lockbox from Seb. He began to pour the coins into the machine's grated mouth.

"I hope you checked those," someone said.

We all three turned: a dark-haired interloper. Her cart was full of frozen bags of mixed berries only, and her eyes couldn't help but flick down to Seb. "For wheat pennies, I mean. Did you check? People collect them."

"We checked," Fa lied, then went back to pouring in the coins. When she was gone, he said, "Can no one mind their own fucking business anymore?" The machine displayed the total in bright numbers, climbing higher. "*Wheat pennies. Did you check? People collect them! Did you check? Did you? Did you?*"

Avast: $60.34.

Fa stuffed the receipt into his pocket and said we were splitting—"my treat," despite it being Seb's treat, actually. His find, his treasure. Fa said what Mom would never: "Buy anything."

Seb checked the DVDs in the rental kiosk, old Dreamworks and Disneys, and pointed at *Madagascar*. "Okay, this."

"We can get that crap for free online, boss," Fa said. "Buy anything else."

So we plundered the cereal aisle. We shook soda liters till they fizzed at the seal, then carefully placed them back on the shelves: booby traps. We heard the hungry whale songs of our stomachs as we chose which flavor of chips to buy: all of them. By the time we found Fa in the grog aisle, picking his poison, our feet had blackened from all the floor's hidden grime.

Fa nodded at us, our loot, made us put nothing back. "Getting this for you," he said, pointing with his boot at a green bodyboard, propped up against the shelves. He pulled down a handle of dark rum. "You'll freaking love it. I'll show you how."

We went to the register of an old guy wearing the same blue vest as all the other employees, some lubber. Fa handed him the Coinstar receipt, and he started passing our loot piecemeal through the register's red frizz of lasers. While they were distracted, Seb pocketed gum from the candy display, and so I did too. Of course the dumb lubber noticed. "I see you," he said but seemed to lose himself when he looked at us. Meaning: when he looked at Seb. The lubber didn't know he was staring—at his forehead, his nose, his mouth—everywhere but his eyes. He wasn't meaning to be rude, sure, but who ever is? Maybe Seb was the first person with Down syndrome he'd ever had to talk to.

Fa saw our stuffed pockets. "Put those back."

"Oh, you know," the lubber said. "It's fine, just gum. They can keep it."

"No." Fa's voice snapped the air—a black flag in high wind. I could tell we were going to get a lecture back at the rental. "You can't."

*   *   *

We docked in a strip mall after that. Fa cracked the windows, even though it was drizzling out and full night, told us to sit tight, then skulked into a store that looked like an office. We didn't talk while he was gone, but I could hear Seb chewing gum—how he'd managed to get that past Fa after we'd been caught, I'll never know. He was holding the empty lockbox, which he'd gotten to keep. Fa came back with a paper bag, stapled and bearing a green cross. "Cool cool," he said, "Off we go."

Later, smoke swimming round his skull, he said, "You ever, like, you know, think about the deep web?"

He was drinking ice water from a bowl using a spoon, crunching the cubes. His eyes had turned kraken—whites tentacled red, pupils black as ink. He hit the joint again, squinted, and said, "I probably shouldn't even be telling you this." Then he told us the deep web was kind of like deep water. Wild and lawless, all creepers and unindexed content. Smugglers trading human organs and social security numbers, all pirated. He chewed slowly, pondering something. "Man," he finally said. "I fucking love ice."

We should've been asleep, but Fa hadn't put us down and by then was too stoned to care. We watched him place his head in his hands and cry. Except he wasn't sad, just asleep. And it wasn't we, just me. Seb had gone away. I went looking for him in the bathroom, out on the wind-whipped bluff. I found him passed out on Fa's bed, shirtless like always. The tablet was faceup on his stomach, still playing some muted cartoon. His face and his sabre-cut, the ceiling and the floor, the whole room moonlit from the device, which rose and fell with my brother's gentle breaths.

*   *   *

Seb is my only sibling. We technically went to the same school, but my classes were in the main buildings, and his were in the portables at the edge of campus. Linoleumed rooms where he did basic addition and spelled his name, fingers white-knuckled to the pencil's rubber grip. We only saw each other at home, and even that was just staring at the same screen or eating at the same table. There were better things to do in Trinidad. Seb mixed a whole variety pack of breakfast cereals into a rainbow pulp so sweet it made my tongue tired. More and more, he explored the cove without telling Fa, me tagging along. He found bleach and distilled vinegar under the rental's sink, squeezed the neon nectar out of laundry pods, mixed all this together in a margarita glass with Fa's grog—"for our enemies." He held the brew up to my nose, so that I could smell its poison.

*   *   *

Fa never did get around to showing us how to use that bodyboard. It stormed the next day, and I think he just forgot. Stuck inside, he started pirating shows onto his tablet so we wouldn't bug him while he napped.

"Is this the deep web?" Seb asked.

"This is Pirate Bay," Fa said.

"But are you stealing?"

"You can't steal something you weren't ever going to buy. Basic econ, dude."

The shows were in English, but with Cyrillic captions, low-def like something underwater. Seb and I watched *Planet Earth* for hours. Sea cucumbers and their ten-tongued mouths, shrimp with eyes that saw fifty times more color than people.

"This is boring," Seb said. "How about *Shrek?*"

"Everything's boring here." I was tired of Trinidad by then, I think. Whole hours would pass with me just staring at the stippled ceiling, pretending splotches were clouds. "We should go home. We're not doing anything."

Onscreen, a big squid was eating a medium squid that was eating a small squid. "If food is scarce," the narrator's geezer voice said, "the Humboldt squids will turn on each other."

Seb rolled his eyes. "We don't *have* to watch this."

He opened a new tab and we moved closer together, typed stuff into the search bar, pretended to be eighteen, steered into the deeps. Seb tugged at his waistband without looking away from what was onscreen. Blue lips and arched backs. Us both acting disgusted, us both acting. Hot tubs and infinity pools. Wet hair and long tails swaying just below the bubbles.

Seb muttered something I didn't hear and looked out the fog-blotted windows. If the skies had been clear, he would've seen those faraway sea stacks.

*   *   *

After his nap, Fa took the tablet and told us to entertain ourselves. Seb puffed out his chest once he was gone, scowled—"*Entertain yourselves, swabs.*" We made each other try Fa's grog, gagging on the burn and chasing it with Coke like we'd watched him do. Seb grabbed the lockbox and we entertained ourselves down to the cove.

I could tell he was scheming again from the way he inspected the shells and rocks. When I asked what he was doing, Seb said, "Oh, just looking," dumbing his face, but I saw the way he watched the water. He picked up a mussel shell and stashed it in the lockbox.

People wearing yellow jackets were spearing trash into plastic bags, crushing urchins and tossing them into bloody bins.

"If those guys see you taking stuff, they'll make you put it all back."

"No they won't." He plucked a purple snail off the rock, held it up and waited to see what emerged: the spidered legs of a crab. Disgusted, he chucked it out to sea.

Later he found a starfish missing two of its arms. He stashed it and explained that mermaids were like sharks, preferring life among rocky crevices not far from shore. He'd read about it online. There were whole websites where people posted grainy pictures of mermaid-shaped shapes—"evidence." He said mermaids used echinoderms like money. Urchins were worth the least; sand dollars the most, but those would be out in the deeps. "If we could just get out there." Seb pointed towards the sea stacks. "That's where all the good stuff is." He picked up an empty shell, boring and beige, and even though I knew he wanted better, he still held it up to his ear, then mine. He still made me listen.

*   *   *

It rained again that night, but the weather switched to wind come morning. We watched more shows and ate barbecue chips until noon, until three, until the sun's slow tumble into the Pacific. I watched shadows clot the carpet, bored again. We were in the middle of a movie about a snail who wanted to be a race car. Our search history had turned the banner ads soft-core, selling stuff like underwear and bras, all open mouths and tattered hair.

"Can we watch something, anything, else?" I said. "This is the worst movie ever made."

"Like you could even know that," Seb said. He was holding the lockbox on his lap, pumping his foot. "This is amazing."

"This is garbage," Fa said. I hadn't realized he was right behind us, also watching. "Aren't you glad we pirated? Who the fuck would spend money on this?"

"I know," I said. "It's so bad." I watched Fa to see if he'd give me a glance, a nod, anything. He exhaled loudly through his nose, sipped his grog, then left.

Seb was glaring at me. He turned off the tablet, and I didn't pretend to be sad about it.

"Okay," he said, not exactly to me. "That's all done now."

Then he left, too. I tried not to follow but couldn't think of anything else to do. I went through the rental looking for him, into the bathroom, out to the wind-whipped bluff. I found him again on Fa's bed, holding the bodyboard Fa had bought us. He was peeling off the plastic.

"I'm going down later," he said. "You can come, too, I guess. If you want."

* * *

We took the bodyboard and the lockbox. We tugged up the waistbands of our swimsuits to keep them from sagging as we ran across the sand, wind clawing at our eyes. The cove was deserted, low tide and almost night. That purple lurch between sundown and dark.

"Give the treasure," Seb said, "and the board." I handed over both and followed him into the waves. The rocks were sharp on my feet, but eventually we got deep enough not to feel the bottom anymore. We both grabbed the board and held on.

"That way." Seb pointed to the sea stacks. We paddled out for what felt like forever but was probably only five minutes. They did not grow one bit closer. Only in the water did I realize how far they actually were.

"My legs are tired," I said. "We can't keep going."

"Keep going. We get out there, we get the good stuff."

"But we won't get out there." A wave bucked and we rolled over it. "It's too far."

"Just shut up," he said, and kicked us forward.

There was a splash nearby, and a pulse of water hit my underside. I looked down but couldn't see anything, not even my own legs. "What was that?"

"What was what?"

Something with scales brushed my back.

I grasped the board and tried to climb on. The thing—whatever it was—darted away. I saw a huge shadow cut through the water, a tail. "Watch it," Seb said. "What are you doing?" I was trying to pull my whole self out of the water. I was trying to dunk him and climb onto the board, as if the only way to get higher was if he went lower. After he bobbed up, Seb jerked the board to knock me off, wrapped his legs tight around it. "You're ruining everything!" he shouted. Somewhere in this struggle, the lockbox slipped loose and sank. Then another wave came, the bodyboard launched away, and we were pulled under.

Down below was nothing but kicked-up sand and the squiggled oculus of the surface. I reached for it, but a current yanked me down and keelhauled me along the ocean's craggled floor. I hit something sharp, eyes shut but bursting bright red. I crashed into things so fast I couldn't process the pain of them. I tried swimming, but couldn't. Tried breathing, but couldn't. There was nothing to do but be dragged toward shore.

*   *   *

Seb was fine. He'd grabbed the board and gone back to floating. I saw him out there after I'd washed up hurting so much I could barely move. He caught the next swell and returned to land.

"That was so sick!" He punched the air but stopped when he noticed me lying there.

"Geez," he said.

I couldn't see how wrecked my back was, but I could feel the loose skin and the sting of grit. I reached around to touch the damage, and my hand came back bloody. Seb leaned in to touch me. I moved away.

"You need a hospital, man."

"I'm good." I wiped snot off my chin and forced it to be true. "I only fell because of that thing."

"What thing?" Wonder came suddenly alive in his eyes; in my throat, rage did the same. "Was it a mermaid?"

"It was something real, stupid—like a shark. I don't know."

"If you don't know, then how can you say it wasn't?"

I shoved him into the sand and ran up to the rental before he could pick himself up.

* * *

Inside, I crept to the bathroom, locked the door, and strained to look over my shoulder at myself. Everything stung. There were streaks of blood, stripped flesh, dark needles stabbed into my shoulder. When I tried to pull them out, they broke apart and left splinters lodged so deep I couldn't scratch them loose.

I heard Seb enter the rental. The bathroom door quivered from him trying to open it. I decided that I would scream if he knocked. But he didn't. Instead, I heard him talking in the other room. The knocking came soon after, harder than Seb's would have been.

* * *

Fa took one look at me and got the keys to the car. He told us to put on our shoes. He said everything was fine, chill, "all good," but his eyes tweaked when Seb asked if this was an emergency.

"He's still breathing," Fa said. "That's what matters."

I took a breath, just to make sure.

Seb said, "Where are you going? A hospital?"

"Hunter hit an urchin, man. The poison's all under his skin now. They'll get infected if they don't come out soon—and don't act like you're not coming. Get your shoes."

"But why?" Seb looked at me, and I realized what he must have already: Dude Trip was over. Going to a hospital would end this voyage. "You don't need me there. Just go. I'll stay here. I won't even do anything bad."

I knew he was telling the truth. But Fa didn't seem to notice.

"No, guy." He spoke so differently to Seb than he did to me—a scurvy mouthful of coos, *dude* and *boss* and *bud* and never his name. "Get your shoes. We'll put them on in the car."

Seb went into the bedroom—definitely ticked, but saying nothing. Fa told him he had two minutes to get outside.

Outside, Fa helped me into the front seat. It felt weird to be up there, I remember. How I could see everything right in front of me, or almost. It was getting dark quickly now. I had to lean forward to keep my back from touching the seat. Fa started the engine, and we waited. Fa waited for Seb. I waited for Fa to chew me out for pushing Seb. I was sure he'd ratted on me. But if Fa knew, he didn't say. He just said, "I can't believe you went out there. What were you thinking? Ava's going to flog me when she sees what happened to you. I mean fucking flog me."

"Am I dying?"

He laughed without joy. "You're not dying. But that's a miracle. I can't believe you didn't break something. Imagine if you'd hit your head."

I laid my chest on my legs. Fa looked at the rental, all the lights still on, and groaned.

"Taking his sweet time, of course."

"It was Seb's idea to go out there," I ratted. "I was just going along."

"You can't just *go along*." His voice, quiet, was somehow worse than shouts. "What if he'd gone and fucked himself like you? What? He would've—" He clenched the wheel and stared straight ahead. We still weren't moving.

He said, "You're not the same."

It was getting harder to breathe. I held tight to my legs and tried to open my lungs. I thought of telling Fa about what I'd seen out there, that creature, but I couldn't find a way to make it sound not made-up. Later, after we went to the hospital, after a nurse daubed my back with alcohol, after she pulled the urchin spines out with cold forceps, after we went home, after Fa got his flogging—but before summer ended, before Seb and I went back to our separate classrooms, our separate ways—I searched everywhere online for what species the thing might've been. I never got an answer. I think I knew I wouldn't, even still in Trinidad. There were scary things lurking out there, circling deep below. I could feel them, fear them, be pulled under by them, but none of that meant I could understand them. My breath shucked my throat. And this, Fa noticed.

"Why isn't he here?" He was looking at me like I knew. Like I had the answer. "Where's your brother?"

JACK FORAKER is a writer from Yolo County, California.

Proper Forage

Barbara Litkowski

A drone is a male honeybee. Drones develop from unfertilized eggs and thus carry genetic material from the queen, only. At the end of the season, when the colony no longer needs their reproductive organs, worker bees forcibly expel the drones. Without the colony's support, they starve or die from exposure.

* * *

Anyone who knew Ted would have said he was not a bee person; bees were for trendy boomers, and, although born in 1952, Ted was anything but trendy. He had discovered his passion for bees at the public library, his refuge on the third Wednesday of every month when his wife Celeste's book club deconstructed notable fiction in their living room. That was how he came upon *Bees of the World*, an oversized volume that revealed an intriguing tripartite world: hordes of identical female workers, a handful of male drones, and a single, egg-laying queen. Magnified photographs showed plump, glistening larvae, adults with wings like rippled, antique glass, and hexagonal combs oozing viscid, golden honey. The more he read, the more he longed to understand the mysteries of the hive, completely at odds with capitalism, democracy, and traditional Western religions.

51

The CO-Z Bee starter kit he purchased on Amazon arrived in three cardboard cartons. Over Celeste's protestations, he assembled the cedar box and pinewood frames and positioned it at the rear of the property where their daughter Lily's playhouse used to stand. From a distance, rising from the fresh-cut grass, the hive resembled nothing so much as a runaway chest of drawers that had encamped on the lawn for a Woodstock revival. Up close, it was a fine piece of craftsmanship, each dovetailed joint reinforced by a wooden peg. A package of mixed bees and an Italian queen, an exotic term for a basic breeder, arrived a week later in separate shipments via special delivery. He named the queen Carlotta. She was larger than all the others, a soft yellow beauty with a glistening thorax and voluptuous tapered abdomen befitting her rank. He installed her with trembling fingers, affixing her traveling cage to a place of honor in the center of a brood frame.

"What if they sting you?" Celeste asked.

"They won't," he assured her. "I know how to handle them."

They *did* sting him. Time after time after time. Despite a cornucopia of training videos and a protective suit, hat, veil, and gloves, also purchased on Amazon, they attacked the crevices in his armor like heat-seeking missiles. Undaunted, he slathered the itchy welts with pink calamine lotion and bore them with pride, emblems of his initiation into the arcane fraternity of apiculture. Celeste registered them in I-told-you-so silence.

Now in his third summer, Ted considered himself a pro (or at least a seasoned amateur) having successfully wintered his original bees and added a second hive ruled by Eleanora. Beekeeping played to his strengths: patience, intelligence, perseverance, and attention to detail. Since retiring, he'd had plenty of time on his hands, and he used it to construct a series of raised beds in the backyard, planting lavender, phlox, snapdragons, cosmos, and sweet peas for the workers. From the comfort of a lawn chair, he observed and recorded his bees' comings and goings with the scientific ardor of an E. O. Wilson. Nights, during down time, in a more frivolous vein, he made up character sketches. To be sure, worker bees were physically indistinguishable from one another, but their personalities were quite different. There were bold Adas who rolled in pollen with happy abandon, timid Sylvias who hovered and sipped, and angry Ruths who flew at his face whenever they spotted him watching. He would have been happy to live the rest of his life behind binoculars. Alas, Celeste had other plans for their golden years. Midwestern winters were too cold for her, and she longed for temperate ocean breezes and an active senior lifestyle. Gulf Sands' Golden Acres on Anna Maria Island fit the bill, offering tennis, water aerobics, a wine bar, two full-service restaurants, yoga, and "life enrichment" classes on everything from cuneiform to edema management. Plus, purchase of a Gulf Sands' property included the vaunted privilege of being bumped up (at minimal cost) to the Chambered Nautilus, an assisted living facility at the rear of the property discreetly screened by oleanders. Ted preferred bees, who just booted you out of the hive when the time came.

Still, after thirty years of marriage, acquiescing to Celeste was like sneezing at the sun, a dry reflex. The couple applied and their offer was accepted. The bad news was that he would have to get rid of his bees. He found a buyer in California, a reputable apiarist offering a good price upon delivery. Transport was a sticking point. Both spouses knew his reflexes weren't what they used to be. Despite Celeste's urging to post notices on local college bulletin boards advertising for a driver, he put his foot down, promising to make the journey in easy stages. "After all we've been through, I owe it to them. You don't need to come with me. I can do this on my own," he added, as much for his benefit as hers.

* * *

The Midwest. The truck had been a pleasant surprise, a boxy rental, more van than truck with smooth white flanks, aerodynamic profile, and free satellite radio. The rear doors opened into a silver cavern with a waffled metal floor that provided ample space for his hives. It had been almost fifty years since he'd driven a panel truck for Erdman's Bakery the summer between his junior and senior years in college, so he took the first hundred miles cautiously, adjusting the rental's mirrors, testing the torque. After that he sped up. Without Celeste beside him there were no tedious podcasts, no white-knuckle admonishments to slow down, no annoying *click, click, click* of knitting needles from the passenger seat. He whistled and sang and bought candy with every fill up. He felt alive, bucking and wheeling like a kite on a string, unspooling.

The first night at the motel when he climbed into the back of the truck to check the cargo, he could feel the bees thrumming gently. After testing the elastic straps, he patted the top of each pine box and said good night. It was cool now, and they were safe. Afterward, he phoned Celeste to let her know he was okay. If only she could share his newfound sense of adventure; instead, what followed was a tepid exchange of marital minutia. Was traffic heavy? Yes, there were more trucks on the interstate than usual, and he was thinking of adjusting his route to avoid them. Did he know that he had left his cell phone on the kitchen counter? Yes, that's why he was calling her from the motel phone. Her final query, "Did you remember to pack your Pepto-Bismol?" fell on deaf ears.

"You'll be glad to know the bees are okay. It's been difficult for them, but they're resilient."

There was a long pause that might have been a sigh. "I miss you," she said at last.

"I miss you, too," he echoed.

Later, after consuming the greater part of a medium pepperoni pizza, a poor cousin of the glossy advertisement on the faux wood credenza, he brushed his teeth and climbed into bed. For years, he had struggled to fall asleep, tormented by earworms, bits and pieces of songs from the sixties. Not tonight. Foregoing his usual side of the bed, he sprawled spread eagle, dead center, asleep in minutes.

*   *   *

The Great Plains. Tired of high-speed traffic, he left the interstate after Oklahoma City, anxious not only to escape the steady stream of semis and tankers, but also eager to get closer to the land itself. At first the novelty of each new place with its indigenous water tower, cinema marquee, and Main Street diner amused him, but after a while, the same pitted curbs, For Sale signs, payday lenders, chain-link fences, and sagging traffic signals made him sad, and so he was relieved when the mileage between settlements increased and people gave way to cattle. Here, at least, he could pretend that the wide-open spaces still promised the chance of the American Dream.

That night, while he waited for a sausage pizza to be delivered, he ambled to a convenience store across the street and bought a couple of six-packs. Dinner arrived as he was draining the first can. In a fit of spontaneous generosity, he tipped the driver a twenty and then tuned to the adult movie channel. After the show he didn't brush his teeth. The next morning, he tossed his disposable razor into the trash.

* * *

New Mexico. Perspective here was different. With the truck's nose pointed due west, he was racing toward a distant vanishing point. The sky, no longer static, was a flickering dance of clouds and colors that squeezed his chest like a carpenter's vise. Disoriented, he felt the need to reach over and touch Celeste's solid, reassuring thigh, to find a fixed point in this reeling world. "What's today's challenge?" he would ask, reverting to a game they had played to pass the miles when Lily was young and fractious, and Celeste would say, "Who can spot the first long-horned steer?" And he would feel safe again. Only there was no Celeste. Just him and the sky and the bees.

* * *

What was that up ahead on the right next to the road? It could be anything. A signpost or a telephone pole or a flowering yucca. Lately, his vision had been playing tricks on him, not just here, but at home, where a flutter in the corner of his eye would scuttle away like a palmetto bug exposed to light. Not today. As he barreled past the target at eighty miles per hour it solidified into a woman with shopping cart.

"What the hell?" he asked the dash, his sounding board in Celeste's absence. The rear-view mirror confirmed it: a suntanned woman in a turquoise tank top and long flowing skirt. A college student, maybe? But then, what on earth would a college kid be doing out here in the middle of nowhere? His conscience goaded him to turn around and see if she was okay; caution advised otherwise. This was a deserted stretch of road and he was an unarmed man in his sixties. What if she was a decoy for a gang of highway bandits? If only he had his cell phone. By now the hitchhiker, if that's what she was, had disappeared into the receding haze. Ahead, the horizon beckoned. Above the whir of the air-conditioner, he heard Celeste urging him to press on, arguing that someone better equipped to deal with emergencies would come along soon. She was undoubtedly right. However, if that person turned out to be a serial killer who targeted vulnerable coeds with shopping carts and long skirts . . .

*   *   *

She was still there.

He made a U-turn and pulled up beside her, leaving the motor idling as a precaution. When he got out, heat punched him in the face. From a distance, the buttes and mesas had looked soft and inviting, their pastel faces smoothed by millennia of weather and erosion. Up close the soil was stark and gritty, crisscrossed by dry gullies. A scattering of succulents, a few sprawling shrubs with flat, gray leaves, and the occasional stunted Joshua tree were the only signs of life. Against this arid backdrop, the woman's skirt was a mandala of russet and topaz and aquamarine. Her wiry blonde hair was banded in a ponytail.

"You okay?"

"Grand." She was wearing sunglasses that gave her iridescent purple iguana eyes.

"Are you sure?"

In one smooth move she shook out her hair and recaptured the ponytail higher on her head. "Yup."

He debated asking where she was going and why she didn't have a car, but his natural reticence prevailed, and he climbed back into the car. "Okay then, I'm off."

"Although, to be honest, I wouldn't mind cooling off in your AC . . . just for a minute."

His stomach knotted and the pizza logjam that had formed in the absence of his usual morning bran shifted. She didn't look threatening or crazy; she looked like Lily at six years old, parading around the living room in her Halloween gypsy costume. He half-expected her to spin like a top, her skirt rising and falling in rolling waves around her ankles, chortling, "Trick or treat!" She slid in on a wave of salt and sweat and female musk that bore no resemblance to Celeste's brisk hand cream. Sweat darkened her tank top. She bent over the air-conditioning vent, plucking the wet fabric away from her body to dry it. The curve of her breasts and the proximity of her hips awakened unsettling, although not unpleasant, sensations he had not felt in years.

* * *

Honeybee mating generally takes place between twenty-five to one hundred feet in the air at top speed. Drones mate in drone congregation areas (DCAs) with queens from different hives bringing fresh genetic material to the hive.

* * *

Today was Wednesday. Back home, Celeste and her bibliophile groupies were nibbling Danish and dissecting some hapless protagonist's poor choices. Who was it this week: Raskolnikov, Clyde Griffiths, Peter Rabbit? He slid his eyes over to the woman on his right. His first impression had been wrong. She was no teen. She had the prominent knuckles of a woman in her late twenties or early thirties. The hair on her arms, bleached by the sun, stood out in a white thicket against her tanned skin. She had pushed the sunglasses onto her head to reveal eyes the color of varnished oak. Her ears lay close to her head and were, surprisingly, unpierced. Up close she looked nothing like Lily, now a thirty-three-year-old dentist with a thriving practice in Vermont.

She wiped the back of her neck and grimaced. "You wouldn't have anything to drink on you? I'm parched."

"I've got some water in the back."

"Awesome."

He shut off the engine and pocketed the keys. He might be old, but he wasn't senile. Going around to the back of the truck, he unlocked the doors, parted a curtain of insulating plastic strips, and clambered into the low-ceilinged, refrigerated chamber. To his left, his veiled beekeeper's hat hung on a peg above a wooden crate filled with scrapers, brushes, and feeders. Keeping his head low, he moved to his hives. "Sorry, about the delay," he said, patting the top of the nearest hive, ignoring Celeste's imagined eyeroll. "We've hit a bit of a snag."

Talking to his bees had started soon after he bought the first hive. "Let's see what you've been up to?" he'd ask, gently removing a honey-soaked frame, or, "Time to batten down the hatches, ladies," closing the entrance before a storm. Over time conversations had grown more personal, with him revealing his growing fear of dying and confessing that, after retirement, his life had felt purposeless until he acquired them. More recently he had told them how sorry he was that he had to sell them, but that it was necessary to preserve his marriage. Now, his fingers absorbed the soothing, familiar thrum of bees chilled into submission.

"There you are. Did you forget about me?" The metal floor vibrated as the woman hoisted herself aboard. Spotting the cooler, she dived for it, surfacing with a plastic water bottle. "Oh. My. God." The cartilage in her throat shivered as she drank. Watching her, Ted found himself enthralled by the rhythm of her swallows and the intimate triangle of flesh under her jaw. A small, irregular mole on her collarbone rose and fell on the tanned sea of her chest. Looking up to meet a pair of polished eyes, he blurted the question that had been troubling him ever since he saw her. "What's a young woman like you doing out here in the middle of nowhere? All by yourself, I mean."

Her body tensed, suddenly wary. "What's it to you?"

Oh, no. She thought he was a pervert or a predator, a marauding wasp or wily skunk with his eyes on the hive. Embarrassed, he backed away until his shoulders collided with the chilled wall. "It's dangerous, that's all." Pinned, with no place to go, he felt her eyes travel from his stooped shoulders and less than imposing pecs all the way to his Velcro sneakers. The verdict showed in her face: harmless.

She relaxed into something resembling comradery. "Hah. You're telling me. Lethal is more like it." She jerked her head in the direction of the cooler. "Do ya mind?" Without waiting, she helped herself to one of the green apples Celeste had packed as a healthy snack. "How about you?" She wiped her fingers on her skirt. "What brings you this far from suburbia?"

He gestured toward the hives, "My gals and I are on our way to California. I've got a buyer for them lined up in San Bernardino."

The oaken eyes narrowed. "*Gals?*"

"*Apis mellifera.* You probably know them as honeybees. They're my hobby—or my obsession—depending on who you ask." He chuckled. "My wife refers to them as my harem because I spend so much time with them." Her stony face revealed his mistake. "Don't get me wrong," he backtracked. "I have the utmost respect for my brood."

The bees had gotten louder, roused by the sound of voices and an influx of heat through the plastic. "Can't you hear them?" she asked, cocking her head toward the hives. "They're unhappy—angry—cooped up like that. They want to be free."

In Ted's experience, ordinary people didn't hold much sympathy for bees, so he found her concern touching. Too bad it was misplaced. Bees *needed* a benevolent keeper to feed them, clean their hives each spring, and test them for mites and disease. "It's for their own good."

"That's what they all say." Glancing back at the hives she shuddered. "You know what? I could use a *real* drink." Her third foray into the cooler produced a couple of chilled beers. Smiling, she sank to the floor and leaned against the wall. Stretched to their fullest, her legs ended in a pair of dusty combat boots. She held up a can and patted the seat beside her.

"Can't," he demurred, "I'm driving."

"Sure, you can. A big bee rancher like yourself. You deserve a treat." She pulled the tab. Foam rolled over the lip and down the aluminum sides, cold and inviting.

What harm could one beer do? With some minor orthopedic maneuvering, he lowered himself to the floor beside her.

"Now, tell me more about your gals." When she knocked her boots together, a cloud of dust erupted.

He took a long pull on the beer. What to talk about? Except for Lily, he hadn't chatted with a young woman in years. The alcohol provided inspiration. "Well," he began, "I'll bet you didn't know that mead, the first alcoholic beverage ever invented, is made from fermented honey. The ancient Greeks called it the nectar of the gods because they thought it bestowed divine powers."

Several digressions later during an account of the Reverend Lorenzo Lorraine Langstroth's struggle to patent the first movable frame beehive in America, the woman's eyes closed, and her left shoulder slid down the wall toward him. He scooted closer, bracing her body with his own. Sighing, she settled her head on the shelf of his collarbone and he put his arm around her tanned shoulder. Her wrist was so narrow he could have encircled it with one hand. Maybe it was being inside a truck again, albeit one without floor-to-ceiling loaves and buns and English muffins, that took him back to the summer when Peggy Washburn was the love of his life, years before he met Celeste. After a day spent stocking shelves, he would take Peggy to the movies, where, under cover of darkness, he would slide his hand under her long-sleeved jersey (theaters were always freezing—just like this truck) and be rewarded with the feel of her soft, warm skin. The woman beside him was much more scantily clad. A strap of her tank top had slipped, and he slid a finger under the fabric and repositioned it on her shoulder. Salt rimed her mouth like a margarita, and he felt an overwhelming urge to lick it off.

The truck's walls cancelled all outside noise creating an artificial world: remote, self-contained, unreal. He assumed cars and trucks were zooming past in both directions, although, ironically, nobody stopped to ask if they needed help. Later, when the journey was over, he would ask himself whether he should have made more of an effort to flag down a car and offload his passenger, but at the time, it had seemed an innocent interlude, an unmarked way station on the map between point A (home) and point B (San Bernardino). The woman stirred and he guiltily pulled his arm away. "Wake up," he said, shaking her. "It's time for me to hit the road."

She blinked, then yawned. "Okay."

And then, because Peggy Washburn had had yellow hair too, he added. "You know, you can ride with me as far as the next town. It wouldn't be any bother, in fact, I'd enjoy the company."

"That would be grand."

On the count of three, they hoisted the supermarket cart into the back of the truck. At close range, Ted saw a roll of chicken wire, an empty birdcage, a duffel bag, a plaid blanket, plastic wading pool, axe, and miscellaneous tubs and shoeboxes. Remembering his harem blunder, he bit back a joke about women and shopping.

Once underway, the woman removed her boots and peeled off her socks. The musty smell increased, and Ted turned up the fan. After gently massaging her feet, she swung them onto the dash. Light filtered through the filmy skirt, silhouetting the oblique angle of her legs. "I'm Oona, by the way." She held up a restraining hand. "And don't say that's an unusual name. That's what everybody says, and it drives me crazy. My parents were big silent movie fans. They named me after Charlie Chaplin's fourth wife, Oona O'Neill."

"More interesting than Ted."

* * *

They had just passed a faded billboard for a McDonald's a hundred miles ahead when he felt a seismic shift in his lower abdomen. The pizza logjam had finally broken. "Sorry," he apologized, "I have to make a quick pit stop." He swerved to the side of the road and braked. "Stay cool. I'll be back in a flash."

The terrain was rough and uneven, and his hands and legs were shaking by the time he reached an outcropping of tumbled boulders, the only privacy in the otherwise open wasteland. Despite the heat, cold sweat beaded his forehead as he dropped his trousers and squatted. At first, he registered nothing but relief, but as his bowels calmed, he noticed a tiny hillock of sand, recognizable from photographs as the entrance to a digger bee's underground burrow. He had read about Southwestern desert bees—there were thousands of species—and seen pictures of their habitats. When a second spasm came, he visualized the burrow's architect, a solitary female—nothing like voluptuous, cosseted Carlotta, or him, for that matter, both fragile foreigners relying on others to survive. He imagined the digger clawing and biting her way through the earth, lining the walls of the tunnel with waterproof secretions from her body. If he were to follow, he would find an egg at the bottom of the hole and provisions to nourish a growing larva. In his mind, he lay curled in that safe, underground chamber ignoring the wretched man above.

Only after the pain subsided, did he struggle to the surface, light, giddy, reborn. Overhead a ghost moon floated in the icy blue stratosphere. If he lay down, he could fashion an angel in the red grit, the way he had as a child, in snow. *Grand.* Oona had said she was "grand." He wanted to be grand, too. "Don't be an idiot, Ted," Celeste barked in his head. "Get up and do something about that woman in your truck."

The first thing he noticed as he retraced his steps was that the truck's rear doors were open. Oona must be foraging in the cooler for more snacks. It was his fault, he supposed, for leaving the motor running. Still, he didn't like the idea of her pungent pheromones and booted tread agitating his gals, already on edge from days of confinement. Picking up the pace, he broke into a ragged trot. He was almost back when a fifty-pound CO-Z hive nosed its way through the insulating plastic strips moving under its own power like a car in an automatic car wash. And then he saw her. Oona. One shoulder pressed to wood.

He froze. "Hey! Wait. What are you doing?"

She raised her head. "I *told* you. They want to be free."

"You can't do that. Bees like mine can't survive out here."

"They're not yours. You've commercialized them. You and society."

She was wrong, of course. Emancipation meant death for his bees. Without proper forage (flowers, alfalfa, and clover) his Adas and Sylvias and Ruths would starve, that is if they were lucky enough to escape the legions of predators. "You've got me all wrong. I take care of them. I care *about* them." Sweat ran down his neck. Why was she doing this? What had he ever done to her except offer her water and a lift?

"She wants money"—Celeste's voice again—"It's that simple."

He had started his journey with one hundred dollars in his wallet. Now, after fast food, candy bars, and generous tipping, all that remained were a couple of twenties. "I don't have much cash on me," he called, patting his pockets in hopes of convincing her. "But it's all yours if you leave them alone." He hesitated. "And if that's not enough, I'll send you more when I get to California."

"Really, Ted." Celeste sighed. "And just what mailing address do you plan to use?"

Oona closed her eyes and laid one divining palm on the hive, remaining transfixed for so long that Ted, inching forward, began to hope that this strange bee whisperer was, indeed, a mercenary charlatan. Instead, the ponytail lashed a violent no. "Keep your dirty money. They're telling me they want their lives back."

The hive missed him by inches. Oona was a strong woman, and her push sent the wooden tower sprawling a yard or so from the tailgate. Miraculously, the joints and entrance seal held. Muttering a heartfelt thanks to the CO-Z craftsmen, Ted moved to inspect the damage. Up close he could see that his gals would need a new hive when they reached California. Still, for now, they were safe. He dropped to his knees and began to stroke the wood, crooning softly.

Oona's rainbow skirt billowed like a parachute as she leaped to the ground. "Out of my way, old man." The axe's first blow glanced off one of a reinforced cedar corner. Its second, aimed at the back panel, struck home.

Raskolnikov, Griffiths, Peter, and Peggy all shouted together, "Don't be a hero. Run!" Lurching away from this axe-wielding fury, Ted scrambled into the truck, where, safely behind plastic, he watched a disaster unfold.

The bees emerged slowly at first and then faster, pouring from the hive's jagged openings in waves. Some particularly athletic insects clung to the axe's blade; others headed for the sun in looping spirals. Oona had dropped the axe and retreated a few paces to observe her handiwork: thousands of angry bees released without any preparation or planning. If he had hoped for dismay or remorse, he would have been disappointed. Her face was alight with glee.

* * *

When a honeybee stings it releases a pheromone that warns other bees of danger. Thus aroused, bees will defend their territory by attacking the perceived enemy. Ten to eleven stings per pound of human body weight are usually enough to cause death in adult males and females.

* * *

Carlotta must have escaped the wreckage and taken refuge in a nearby creosote bush because a pulsing brown sack knitted from thousands of bees now dangled from a crooked branch by a living umbilical cord. The only swarms Ted had seen before were on training films. Those controlled migrations, he knew, were nature's way of responding to overcrowding within the hive. They usually occurred in the late spring or early summer when the bees were well-fed and not aggressive. This exodus was different—violent and unpremeditated. He could only hope that Carlotta and her court would remain docile. The frantic stragglers, however, were an unknown quantity. Hundreds of them remained on high alert circling the damaged hive, primed to strike.

Don't do anything you'll regret later had always been Ted's mantra, and he intended to follow it now. He didn't regret wheeling the shopping cart through the plastic curtain and launching it into the bee-infested desert where it hit the ground, bouncing twice before it flipped on its side, crushing the plastic wading pool and sending cardboard tubs rolling haphazardly in all directions. Nor did he regret donning his full beekeeping armor to ward off stings as he made his escape. Godlike in white hat and veil, he clambered down from the cargo bay. By this time Oona had left her observation post and was gathering her belongings, repacking them in her cart, oblivious to the heightened insect activity. She looked up when she heard the cargo doors slam. In the bright light, her skin looked scoured and pitted. The purple iguana glasses were back in place making her eyes inscrutable. She gave him the merest of nods and then turned away, swatting aimlessly at nearby Ruths.

"Don't swat," he called over his shoulder in passing. "It only makes them mad. If one stings you, run like hell." She made no move that she had heard him. Once inside the safety of the cab, he lowered the window and tossed out the veil and gloves.

He left her as he had found her, standing alone by the side of the road. He did not stop at the next town, or the next, or the one after that. He had paid a steep price for his indiscretion, and he had no desire to reveal it to others. Half his bees were as good as dead, their former home destroyed. As the truck sped west, he imagined night falling. Owls would take to the sky and coyotes and kit foxes would creep from their burrows and feast on the hive's wooden flanks, glutting themselves on the sticky manna that had miraculously bloomed in the desert. Weeks would pass and the unrelenting sun would bleach the pinewood frames into yet another desert skeleton, idle speculation for passing motorists.

*   *   *

That night on the computer in the airless cubbyhole the motel called a communications center, he searched for "woman in desert with shopping cart." There was a woman cycling across the country to raise awareness for breast cancer and an unidentified immigrant's body had been found somewhere near the southern border, but neither of them was his woman. After a while, he gave up and logged off. When he got home, he would have to tell Celeste that he'd misunderstood the original terms of sale and she couldn't have the bedroom suite she'd had her heart set on for their new home.

BARBARA LITKOWSKI *holds an MFA in Creative Writing from Butler University. Her short story "Monarch Blue" won Arizona State University's 2018 Climate Fiction Short Story Contest, was anthologized in* Everything Change, Volume II, *and reprinted in the international journal,* IMPACT. *Her short stories have also appeared in* Subtle Fiction, Blue Lake Review *and* Luna Station Quarterly. *She was selected as a finalist in the 2012 William Faulkner-William Wisdom Novel-in-Progress Competition and is a former recipient of the Indiana Arts Commission Individual Artist Program grant. She lives with her husband in Zionsville, Indiana.*

Where the Last Grizzly Was Murdered

Charisse Hovey Kubr

I

Having a grandfather as a judge or being heir to a ten-acre ranch had something to do with why Jay Monroe was hated. He was hated first, right off the bat, for his blond hair, blue eyes and freckles, and then, he was hated more deeply, because Jay Monroe would never back down from a fight.

We met in seventh grade but I had heard about Jay Monroe. The Monroe House legacy was part of the folklore. The did-you-knows . . . Did you know Jay Monroe has been an alcoholic since the age of ten? Did you know he is going to end up in jail just like his dad? Did you know it snows on Saddleback Mountain? Did you know Black Star Canyon is haunted by angry Indians? Did you know Old Lady Irvine kills anyone who trespasses Irvine Ranch at night?

We had English class with Dr. Stein. Jay showed up to the first day of school with a black eye. He had scabs all over his arms. He sat next to me. When Jay smiled, his grin scrunched up his freckled cheeks, blocking his eyes. The skin on his black eye was green and yellow and purple and pink. I guess *black eye* is a figure of speech. Dr. Stein was the only teacher with a *Dr.* in front of his name at our public school. I couldn't imagine why a doctor worked as an English teacher at a junior high school that sat smack in the middle of the barrio. Our school sheltered a mix of Mexican kids and kids who rode thirty minutes on a school bus because their parents wanted to be on county land, not in a city.

I imagined Dr. Stein in a glass high-rise hospital with well-dressed people. Not with us.

We wore clothes covered in fur from the morning feeding and manure on our shoes. We pretended to have sharpened pencils. No one would give up a pencil. You'd never get it back.

Dr. Stein had this idea to have students work during zero period as peer tutors. He said it will look good on a college application. He held an essay competition. All three of his seventh-grade classes wrote the essay as a required assignment. Jay Monroe and I were the only two selected out of over a hundred kids. We were not the A students. We were just as surprised at being chosen, as the A students were at not being chosen. Whatever our essays contained, it was exactly what Dr. Stein was looking for. He had his glass-tower ideas.

II

The Monroe House was ancestral, rooted into the igneous granite rock forming the foot of Saddleback Mountain. A chain-link fence bordered the property and was burdened by orange trees leaning, old blackberry bushes with horned vines weaving, and a dapple-gray horse prying her head under the fence, reaching with muscled lips toward the wild overgrown weeds on the other side. For years, the fence was bent that way, with archways made by horses to grab at the plants. At twilight, coyotes passed through the arena like silent gray winds. After dark it was easy passage for raccoons who made a mess of the dirt, leaving behind black-tipped fur in the chain links.

On hot days when the sun heated up the dirt covering sage scrubs in powder, the neighborhood dogs would pack up and race through The Monroe House arena, getting chased out by the seemingly lazy dapple-gray mare. They did it for sport, just to get on her nerves, escaping out the archways on the other side, hearing the crush of her hooves. She charged at those dogs and stopped in a cloud of brown dust with a snort. The band of mutts looking back at her through the links, dirt-clodded tongues hanging out.

Everyone called it The Monroe House. It was set on a bend in the road. So, in giving directions, people would say, "Just past The Monroe House" or, "If you get to The Monroe House, you've gone too far." It held the wonder of a landmark; like Saddleback Mountain looked like a saddle and Mount Baldy looked like the head of a bald eagle, The Monroe House looked like Judge Monroe, ancient and reliable as geography.

III

When beholding a mountain, mute in the presence of its greatness, we Californians know the mountain is movable and the faults running through its interior mass are unpredictable. We are faulted by nature. I saw Judge Monroe. I was muted by his power and afraid of what unknown fault lay beneath a face proven trustworthy over time.

I was a trail rider. After school, all I wanted to do was ride out into the hills and try to get lost. I had to ride my horse past The Monroe House to get to the fire-break trailhead.

Judge Monroe stood on a granite outcropping that made a natural ledge separating the lower horse arena and barn from the upper level of the property where the home sprawled out ranch style, one story, painted red matching the barn. He was old and shrunken. Freckles had taken over his face. It was orange as saddle hide. His once blond hair was white. The tips of the white hair were stained yellow from cigarette smoke. Yellow and thick, sticking out under a well-worn felt cowboy hat. By the judge's body language, someone was in trouble. He was giving orders from his perch. The judge's voice boomed, a commanding rumble, like hearing the earthquake before feeling it under your feet.

I saw a boy, about my age, toss a rope around the dapple-gray mare's neck and lead her away from the edge of the arena. The boy's boots, jeans, and flannel shirt were dusty over a crust of dried mud. He had blond hair and red freckles. He bent down, picked up a stone, and added it to what I saw was a small wall he was building. Usually they built those walls to direct water so the arenas wouldn't flood during a rain. He labored as if working off a crime not his own, with humility entering into humiliation. That was Jay Monroe.

I galloped away. The cracking of rocks under my horse's hooves and the rhythm of the clap clap clapping of her steps beat and echoed off the face of The Monroe House and entered the body of the judge, lowering his heart rate.

It wasn't earthquake weather today.

IV

Jay and I tutored Cecelia Lopez. Cecelia's father was the head of the most powerful local Mexican gang. They killed people. We were seventh graders. That's when they initiated their kids into the gang: twelve years old. Every day she was at school, which was not often, she came in for help. Emergency help.

Cecilia came early, right at the beginning of zero period. She looked like she'd been up all night. Her blue hooded sweatshirt and blue chino pants were dirty and wrinkled. Her black eyeliner and eyebrow pencil looked freshly drawn. She plucked out all her eyebrow hair and drew on her brows. She came up to me, pulled a chair, sat backward in it facing me, leaned in, and whispered.

"Eh, Chica. The history paper. You gotta do it," Cecelia said.

"It's due today. Show me what you have," I said.

"I don't have it," she said.

From her back pocket, she pulled out a folded piece of paper. It had the title at the top, her name in the righthand corner. Then over the face of the page, letters were scratched in. It looked like she was trying to write in the dark. Crooked, lightly pressed with the pencil. Something was wrong. We looked at each other in silence. We had this bond, like we could read each other. We really could not conceal ourselves. Uneasy, she undid her messy ponytail, combed her fingers through her hair, and retied a low tight ponytail. She wore a collection of black rubber bands around her wrist like a bracelet. Skillfully, she pulled off the rubber bands one by one and nimbly, quickly, tied them exactly every few inches all the way down her straight brown hair like a rope that sat in her lap.

"Not allowed to do schoolwork. I had to hide. I want to do it. I want to," she said. She was so tired.

"I will tell you what to write," I said. I dictated, she wrote.

Jay was tutoring someone else, but he knew all of what was going on. Cecelia's dad just got out of prison. Everyone was talking about it. Did you know her dad killed his own cousin for not doing what he said? Did you know Cecelia's mom had her when she was so young she never even went to high school? Everyone knew Cecelia's desire to do well in school and not follow in the footsteps of her parents had to be hidden, but Jay judged things differently.

"You are not helping her," yelled Jay across the room. "She has to do it herself!"

Jay was standing up waving his hands. Hollering at us. He turned red and yelled. "When you're gone," he said. "She has to be able to do it alone!"

"Mr. Monroe," said Dr. Stein. "Keep it down, Jay."

"But this isn't right," yelled Jay, loud. You could hear the other classrooms become silent.

Stein knew the direction this was going.

"You can walk yourself to the principal's office," said Dr. Stein.

It must have been the judge in him that would get irate with anything he felt was unjust or unfair. Jay Monroe had a hyperexplosive reaction when it came to knowing the difference between right and wrong and a violent intolerance for anyone who did wrong in his eyes. So, with Jay exploding all over the place, he spent a lot of time in the principal's office.

V

Jay left class, went toward the administration halls, then walked right past the principal's office. He walked off campus, down the middle of the black asphalt street for three blocks and ended up in front of The Lopez House, a bungalow with a large wooden porch that had that 1950s wooden house scent emitting out the doors, down the painted steps and mixed with the dry soil and grass odor. Eight men were working on cars. Old cars parked on the lawn. Some men were inside the house. They wore tan chinos, white tees, and blue Dickey work shirts over.

"Mr. Lopez!" Jay called. "Is Mr. Lopez home?" Jay yelled out to the crowd in general. He stood tall in the middle of the street, not crossing the invisible property line. He fixed his hair, tucked in his shirt.

"What? You Cecelia's boyfriend?" a voice said. Some laughed. Others dropped whatever they were doing and lined up on the lawn like soldiers.

"No. I am her friend. Is Mr. Lopez home?"

"Oh, fre-end," the man said, mocking, making rude gestures.

"He's gone," another man said, holding a wrench. "Get outta here." Three of the men, one with a chain in his hand, walked toward Jay.

"I want to talk to him," Jay said.

"Go home," a man wearing a white wife-beater tank top said. He shoved Jay. Jay bounced back and went right up to the man's face.

"I know he's in there," Jay said. "I just want to talk to him. I can see him inside." Jay called out toward the house, "Mr. Lopez! I see you in there!"

The man punched Jay in the stomach. Horses had kicked him and knocked the wind out of him many times, so Jay knew the sensation would pass. After unbending himself, Jay forced his way, walking sideways across the lawn up to the porch.

"Cecelia is smart," Jay yelled at the house. "Give her a chance. She is smart, do you hear me!"

His words vibrated over the hardwood floor inside the house, reaching Mr. Lopez. "She is smart, give her a chance!" Jay yelled again. Four men grabbed Jay, carried him off, and threw him in the middle of the street on the other side of the invisible territory line. Mr. Lopez appeared in the doorway to get a load of this kid. He watched Jay stand up and walk straight down the middle of the street back to school.

Later, in woodshop class, Jay was picking black asphalt out of his elbows—parts of the street in front of Cecelia Lopez's house formed a small pile on Jay's desk.

VI

Everyone knew you had to stick with the crowd walking to lunch or you'd get jumped. Everyone knew you never went into the girls' bathroom. I was late for lunch and walked alone down the hall. Aida, one of Cecelia's gang members, showed up out of nowhere and followed me.

"What you lookin' at, ugly?" Aida said to me.

"Hi, Aida," I said.

"I asked you who you lookin' at?"

She shoved me against the wall, pinning my shoulders and chest to the wall with her arms. She pressed a knife against my shoulder. I felt pressure under the metal blade.

"Aida," I heard a voice call. It was Cecelia.

Aida looked at Cecelia in fear, as though she was caught doing something wrong. "She's cool," Cecelia told Aida.

On Cecelia's word, I was released. Aida could not touch me because it would have been disrespectful to Cecelia if she did. Cecelia was a Lopez. Her dad killed anyone who crossed him. So, Aida tried to laugh it all off as if it were a joke, saving her own hide.

"Ha, ha. Cecelia say you cool, you cool," Aida said to me. She put her knife back in her sock and walked away laughing. "Hey, why don't you do my homework too," Aida said. "Ha, ha." I checked out my shoulder. I was bleeding but not bad.

"Don't worry about her, Evie," Cecelia said. "She's crazy. Doesn't mean nothin'."

"Why would she do that," I said, "I didn't do anything to her. I wasn't looking at her."

Cecelia took the blue bandana out of her pocket, folded it, then pressed it to my shoulder, applying pressure as though she'd done this before.

"Doesn't mean nothin'. It's initiation. She has to cut someone. It's over now. She won't do it again."

Aida called back at us from the end of the hall. "You think she's your buddy Cecelia? Tell me when she has you over to her house. Tsss. You watch out Mija." Aida went back to laughing.

"Chhh. Forget her. She's crazy," Cecelia said. "You an' Jay are cool. You don't have to worry about nothin'."

We looked at each other in silence. I could read her. I knew she knew what Jay had done at her house. Standing up to her dad. I knew grades were important to Cecelia and I was helping her get good ones. Without saying so, Cecelia realized me and Jay had her back, and it was the first time someone outside her gang showed they cared. She was repaying us within her power. Giving us protection. She slowly pulled the bandana from my cut. The bleeding had stopped.

"I'm good, huh?" she said, seeing the blood had stopped. "I'm gonna get into that nursing program at the hospital, the candy stripers," Cecelia said. "They give you a cool uniform."

She walked off and joined her gang who sat on the far slope of the field. She sat with Armondo. Mondo was a football player who wanted a college scholarship. He was short but quick and ran a lot of touchdowns. At games, people chanted Mon-Do! Mon-Do! He changed out of his football uniform before going home and back into his white wifebeater. He hid his jersey in a bag behind a bush every night and picked it up every morning on the way to school.

Cecelia told me about her and Mondo one day during tutoring. "For initiation," she said, "we were supposed to do it. But, me and Mondo. We went into the room. Hung out for a while. And when we went out, we told everyone we did it."

Later, the gang found out. They couldn't punish Cecelia, she was a Lopez. Time went by. The local paper wrote an article on Mondo. His photo wearing the football uniform, scouts had approached him, a local success story. With the story still on the stands, Mondo was shot in the chest while walking home from Moreno's market one night. Everyone said it was an initiation kill. They told some kid to shoot that guy right there walking out of Moreno's market. It was Mondo. The twelve-year-old killer had no idea at the moment he killed his own blood.

VII

Toward the end of the school year, the sun doesn't set until after nine o'clock at night, so it was a good time to go out to the waterfall before it dried up for summer. Jay and I were both trail riders, so we decided to meet out on the fire road and head out for the falls. He rode a huge horse with a back like a couch. I rode our quarter horse who could get to the falls and back with her eyes closed.

The fire road narrowed into a coyote trail. Chaparral and sage brushed against us, bursting with fragrance. This part of the ride got so hot, you'd get impatient to reach the water, cool off, and rest. Then you hear the waterfall before you see it. There's a big open area, maybe where the pond was a lake thousands of years ago. Now, the water falls down into a green pond. This exact location, the pond, is blood-soaked land. The last California grizzly bears were killed here by the hunters. The Native tribes battled the Spaniards, the American fur trappers battled the Mexican caballeros, the famous Judge Monroe put the wrong people in prison, saving the hides of the land gamblers who murdered men over a one-dollar bet. And still, the ghost of Old Lady Irvine keeps all the lovers from taking night drives into the empty Black Star Canyon mines.

We reached the pond and Jay rode his horse right in. That big white horse clearly loved the water. In the deep part, his horse swam around, taking pleasure in swimming with Jay holding on to the mane. Jay put his head under and let his horse drag him through, the water moving over him. When his horse touched ground, he righted himself above so his legs straddled back as they rose out of the water on dry land. On the other side, he slid off and let the horse play in the water. He didn't need to tie up this horse. He stayed near Jay like a loyal dog. I took my horse's bridle off so she could graze.

"Hey," Jay said. "We should bring Cecelia out here."

"I don't know," I said. "How?"

"That would piss 'em off," he said.

"She could ride double with me," I said.

Jay, dripping wet in his jeans, climbed up a granite boulder and dried off in the sun. He rung out his shirt and hung it on a tree limb. His horse grazed. I remembered what Aida said, how I would never have Cecelia over to my house. Jay would. Jay did. He was planning it all out up there on his drying rock. On this blood-soaked land, Jay schemed of love. He judged the blood of the past as fertilizer for the future.

VIII

This was his plan. Jay decided Cecelia would take the late bus home with me after school. The day Cecelia took the bus home with me was hot. She wore her gang uniform, white wifebeater tank top, black bra, chino pants. The bus driver eyed her. He didn't want a gang member on his bus. I said she was going home with me.

He let her ride but kept looking at her in the mirror. She looked right back at him with her heavy black eyeliner, brown skin dewy in the heat.

Cecelia had never seen a horse before. In the barn, each time the animals would stomp, whinny, snort, bang against the stall, swish their tails, bite at a fly, she was uneasy.

"I don't got stuff to wear," said Cecelia.

"We go barefoot sometimes," I said. She looked at the hooves.

"Chhh." Cecelia shook her head. "Can't I ride that one over there?" she said, pointing to the pony.

"No one rides that pony," I said. "That pony is dangerous!"

She didn't trust me. "It's little."

"Believe me," I said. "Most of the time the big horses are safer."

"You messin' wit' me?" She glared at me under half-closed lids. Cecelia combed her fingers through the pony's frizzy forelock, pulling rubber bands off her arm and fixing the pony's forelock neat and clean. Her hands moving with the skill of a surgeon.

"We will ride double, Cecelia," I said. "All you have to do is sit there."

"Chhh," she said, shaking her head. Jay said to meet him at the bridge. By the time we got to the bridge, Cecelia was comfortable and didn't hold on to my back.

"Cecelia," Jay said. "Why don't you come over here and I'll teach you how to ride Harley."

"Get outta here," Cecelia said.

"Really, I'm not going to do anything weird. You ought to know the basics. You're here aren't you?"

Cecelia slid off my horse and Jay helped her up on Harley. Jay sat behind her and showed her how to hold the reins, how to turn with the reins, how to use her legs to give cues, then how to stop. She was riding pretty well. We made our way toward the falls.

Riding double, Jay couldn't help himself and he wrapped his arms around Cecelia and sunk into her body, breathing her into his lungs, his psyche, his plans.

"Get offa me," Cecelia said and slapped his arm hard. Unused to holding reins, she dropped them when she had to open her hand to slap Jay, but that made Jay have to lean over her even harder to grab the reins, which was worse for her.

"Evie, I'm going back over with you," she said. Cecelia played hard to get and that drove Jay mad with love.

"Just stay," Jay said. "Look, I'll scoot back here."

Jay moved himself back, putting a few inches of space between his body and Cecelia. He grinned that smile that scrunched up his cheeks and covered his eyes. Cecelia was cold. She wouldn't even look at him. This made him love crazed. We rode out the quiet. Watched hawks and lizards.

"Cecelia," he said. "I haven't seen Aida at school lately. It's like she's dropping out. We only have a couple weeks left."

"You not gonna see Aida," Cecelia said.

"You can talk to her. She'll listen to you."

"She's not coming back."

"She does whatever you say," he said.

"She's not coming back," said Cecelia. "Never coming back to school."

"What's her problem?"

"She don't got no problem, Jay," said Cecelia, hitting him again in the arm. "She's having a baby."

He leaned back, giving her space, still controlling his horse. The rhythm of the horses walking was calming. He looked at me, and I saw on his face the moment he turned from a boy into a man. I watched Jay and Cecelia fall in love in front of my eyes. They had a way of talking to each other. It was English, I heard the words, but somehow, they seemed to be speaking an intimate familial language understood only by the two of them.

Cecelia had that joyous, innocent light in her eyes people get when thinking of babies. Jay would die protecting it.

IX

We swam in the green pool of water. We climbed up the rocks and sat under the loud waterfall, letting it beat on our heads.

We drank from the same spot that attracted the grizzly bears, coyotes, raccoons, the Native tribes, the ranchers, the coal miners, the caballeros, the land gamblers, the judges. The wrongs committed on all sides of our ancestries rinsed. Jay pulled Cecelia up to his favorite rock for drying, a giant granite boulder. Like a metamorphic rock arises from the transformation of existing rocks, Jay and Cecelia were mountain building. They were changing the form of their genetic past. She rung out her hair. Water splattered on the hot granite, evaporating. She put her hand on Jay's head, fluffing the water out of his hair. They kissed each other. Their love dripped down the boulder, filling its faults.

The Monroe House is not set on a bend in the road. The architects of that house are up there drafting plans on the drying rock, tracing patterns with wet fingers over the granite, watching the lines dry up and disappear. Cecelia frames The Monroe House by stitching up bullet holes and knife wounds as they come into the emergency room. She gives them an earful. Jay gives it a movable foundation, naming their company J&C Construction, painting their initials on the side of his truck. He builds anything. The Monroe House is not set in stone.

I hear the packs of dogs barking a few hills over. The heat sits on my skin like a coat fragrant from pond water, the under mud escaping from the horse hooves exposing the deep cool. The leaves of the oaks are still but they are thick and not the best indicators. On the hilltops the overgrown sprouted ends of the mustard plants show no wind, yellow blocks the blue. My horse stops chewing, lifts her head, ears forward.

It's earthquake weather today.

CHARISSE HOVEY KUBR published her first short story as a teenager, earned a bachelor's degree in Creative Writing from California State University at Long Beach and worked as the Editor of Sun Newspapers *in Seal Beach, California. Her freelance creative nonfiction has been published in magazines such as* Sea, The Yacht, Destinations *and the* Orange Coast College Marine Science Journal. *In addition to teaching English Language Arts in public schools, she has taught Creative Nonfiction at Idyllwild Arts Academy, Outdoor Education in Big Bear and once worked as a horseback Interpretive Naturalist in Kings Canyon National Park. Currently she teaches English courses while writing short stories and screenplays in Redondo Beach, California where she lives with her husband and two children.*

Above Snowline

Rachel Markels Webber

For my mother, Joan Malory Webber

In the snow I was kicking steps for Aardvark and Buffalo when something struck me funny. I thought, I've got no name. The mountain falls away. Feet skid through air. I land on snow-covered moss, grab rock, slither up the crevasse. Buffalo reaches his long arm down for mine, his ice-encrusted beard scratches my cheeks as he pulls me back up onto the ledge.

After that they call me Lizard. It seems that was always me. Down below, they call us climbers. Up here, above snowline, we just are. Animals, we call ourselves. The mountains come on and on. By summer's end our eyes grow wrinkled with the laughter and the light. We find a rhythm in one another and in the mountain—each step brings us closer in.

I used to climb alone. I forgot how to talk to strangers, forgot their old-world ways. Words like *he* and *she* became alien, sometimes even *me* and *you*. Coming home from the Rockies before school started last September—before the snow fell—I went a week without talking. Jen made lemon-honey tea while she called my university head and told her I had laryngitis.

More and more now I travel with a pack. We sprint past those northerners with their designer gorp and organic sunscreen. They move as if each step takes some untold effort, crawling slowly up the mountain—yet they are so beautiful with their high cheekbones and burnished skin. I can't help but hope that maybe this time it will be different. Some one of them will understand us—will know our mountain ways. But they are gone by first snowfall. Weeks go by and we speak only to one another other in a language all our own.

It's true things are hard sometimes. Winter returns quickly. The snow never stops. Winter-beaten trees collapse, like lightning down below. Painfully I learn how to walk down slopes, heels flat, toes up. Steep snow frightens me, but I'm Lizard, on rock I flow.

Sleeping at night, in the high country, curled up with Buffalo, I dream of a life in another place where there are streets, cars, offices, sex, money, and books. But these dreams come less often now that the nights are short, and daytime summit sleep is quick and free. In January, buying flannel sheets with Jen at Ikea, I flee to the parking lot.

"I don't know how to be," I tell her when she finds me strapped into the bright blue Prius I thought I'd wanted.

While she drives slowly through Ballard, I hang my head out the window gasping for air.

Later in the barn, I breathe in the sweet smell of manure and fresh pine shavings. Jen's blue eyes hold me as she traces the muscle patterns on the glistening black body of her favorite horse. He leans into her, pushing his weight into her dry calloused hands, as she instinctively stops at each muscle knot, massaging each irregularity. Sometimes I think I can see through her lean scarred hands. Each year, by summer's end the hairs on her arms grow vertical, bright gold.

I trace a tiny scar I've never noticed on her eyelid, gently running my finger over the jagged line, questioning its origin.

"Horse," her voice answers my silence.

"How?"

"Brought his head up and I was in the way. Had to stay in the hospital for a week—some worried I'd lose my vision." Her body contracts in my arms at the memory.

I'm amazed she survived the confinement.

An old lover once told me that I was raised by wolves. We were at an English department cocktail party the day after I'd come back from a climb up Mount Rainier over spring break. My feet were swollen and barely fit into my black suede shoes. I kept scratching at the rayon fabric of my dress pants. Unused to my own voice, I asked leading questions, encouraging my colleagues to do the talking. It didn't matter—my lover always spoke enough for both of us. When she moved out six months later, I barely noticed her absence. I'd been sleeping with Jen for months.

Sometimes in the classroom, I think someone else is speaking, my voice rough and foreign from lack of use. Before Bec came to live with us, Jen spoke less than I. When I'd come home from the mountains, we'd speak in symbols and hand motions, sometimes for days, as we sipped our tea and waited for the silence to break. And it was in that silence that the phone rang late in the winter. My sister Tal, keeper of family secrets and all of my memories, gone—leaving me a beat-up old Volvo, a few hundred bucks, and her twelve-year-old daughter.

* * *

Late at night, after everyone else has gone home, Jen and I stand next to the pine box that holds my sister's body. Wiping the darkness away, I see Tal and me sloping through the forest, stunned and sly, harsh phantoms of ourselves and who we would become. Sometimes we hear what we already know to be true. Halcyon. She'd come home from work, made dinner, cleaned the house, and read a chapter of *The Mists of Avalon* with her daughter, Bec. After Bec fell asleep, Tal poured herself a glass of whiskey, got into bed, and swallowed the entire bottle of pills. In the morning when Bec found her, she left a message at the last number she had for a father who never called her back. It wasn't until nightfall that she'd called us.

"She needs you," Jen says, squeezing my hand.

"Doesn't seem like it." Bec had been quick to depart with an old friend of Tal's. Only a few others, mostly dutiful colleagues of mine who saw my sister's obit in the paper, had shown up for the service. The only other friend of Tal's in attendance, a Buddhist monk Tal had met the year she'd spent in a monastery, had officiated.

"She does. She needs you to be here," Jen says, staring at the wooden box.

Bec arrives the next day with a battered purple suitcase that I remember Tal taking to summer camp, a red Schwinn bicycle, and a calico cat named Jaz who promptly tears a hole beneath the ticking of Becca's box spring and crawls inside. If she could have, Becca would have crawled in with her. She unpacks her few belongings while Jen makes a quick shopping run and brings home peanut butter, white bread, and a box of Ding Dongs.

"You think she'll eat these?" I ask, examining the mile-long list of illegible ingredients on the back of the Hostess package. I open the box to examine these artifacts of my childhood.

"I don't know. When I asked her what her favorite foods were she said she didn't have any."

Jen stands by the counter grating gruyere for a macaroni and cheese recipe she found in a cookbook we discovered in the attic while looking for furniture for Bec's room. I come up behind her and bury my head in her hair, inhaling the sweat smell of lavender. Wrapping my arms around her middle, I pull her in. She puts the grater down and leans back into my chest. We stay there, fitted into each other's bodies until she slowly pulls away.

"Feed the horses?" she asks as she cracks a couple of eggs into a bowl.

When I come back inside, Bec has emerged from her room wearing an old gray hooded sweatshirt that I think was Tal's and a pair of faded blue jeans patched with red calico. She is tossing silverware into seemingly random piles onto the table that Jen and I brought down from the attic yesterday. Jen ladles out the mac and cheese while Bec and I stand self-consciously by the cherry table my grandfather carved as a wedding present for my parents.

"Sit anywhere." Jen smiles hopefully at Becca. Becca plops down in the nearest chair without looking at either of us.

I pull the spoon out of my pile and scoop up a bite of the mac and cheese. I smile at Jen wishing I could reach over the table and kiss her. Bec picks up her fork and pushes the food around on her plate.

"Like peanut butter?" I ask.

"I'm not hungry," Bec murmurs, not looking up from her plate. Her tangled hair has fallen over her face. "Can I go to my room?"

I look at Jen, hoping she'll know what to say.

"Sure," Jen answers. Bec puts her plate on the kitchen counter and looks back at us to see if we are watching. I avert my gaze as she takes a Ding Dong from the open box I left on the counter and heads out to the barn. She's like a feral animal with her long-tangled mane and ragged clothes. My sister's child, she is a part of me. Yet I don't know how to be for her.

She hardly leaves her room except to go to school. Her one-word answers to our inadequate questions barely break the silence we are used to.

At our first parent-teacher conference we are told what we already imagine to be true. Another outcast, a brainy boy named Ricki, is Bec's only friend. At recess she sits in the farthest corner of the playground, knees curled up to her chest, reading a book.

"She's in her own world, oblivious to everything around her," the school counselor tells us.

"What is she reading?" I ask, wanting to know what engrosses her, what transports her from the hell where she feels she has landed. I am met with a blank stare.

"Let's move," I say to Jen later that night after Bec is asleep in the loft.

"Where?"

"Antarctica, the wilds of Alaska, Inner Mongolia . . ."

"Worried about Bec?"

"I just want her to know who she is." I look at Jen, and her blue eyes seem to sparkle in the moonlight that streams through our bedroom window. "I want to know who she is."

In the silence she envelops me in her arms. The warmth of her chest pushes against my breasts as she pulls me closer. When we were two, I wanted nothing more than to climb inside her, to disappear into safety. Now I want nothing more than to take Bec and run away to the mountains. I want her to be safe. I want her to know that I will be there.

Spring arrives and my students dance around the classroom like teenage gazelles. Long and lean, they leap and twirl into the air, throwing their hands wildly toward imaginary baskets—emulating the high priests of the basketball court. When the bell rings, I try to bring them back to the high priests of the English language, a language that I've made my living at, crafting sentences of my own to convey the power of words in the works of Shakespeare, Milton, and others whose works I was once enamored of. But lately I'm only aware of that language's inadequacies. Donne's sermons seem pale in comparison to the magnificence of the SuperSonics.

When the Seattle team wins the national title, even Bec asks for a basketball, which Jen brings home from Dick's. Driving home from the mountains early on a Sunday evening, I see my niece in the schoolyard. Her tangled brown hair is pinned down under a red checkered hat that once belonged to my father. She's wearing patched jeans and a frayed t-shirt that she must have found in the basement from the women's Annapurna expedition. I can't help but smile upon seeing the expedition's motto, *A Woman's Place Is on Top,* written boldly across her flat chest. I pull over behind a tree and step out of the car, wanting to be with her, but not wanting her to see me. In my shirt and my father's hat—Bec is finding her place with us—as we are with her. A pudgy tow-headed boy, who must be Ricki, wearing rolled-up tan chinos and horned-rimmed glasses stands across the hoop from her. Taking turns, they aim their balls at the basket. I can't help but notice that neither ball ever seems to reach its intended destination.

Above tree line, the snow melts, revealing the red and yellow mountain lichen which blankets the summits. We climb a veneer of waterfalls. My hands slip on the spicy-smelling moss as I scramble over rock. It's easy to live here in the high country, especially in spring. We share high ease, shed layers, spread over the rock, climbing skywards like happy lizards. Our bodies rise to turn invisible in the early morning sun. Our faces in the heat are clown white—goggled in black. By summer's end my lips are charred and swollen as old paint. I peer through slits. The sun boils out my veins and I suck on glacier ice for scant relief.

Back in Seattle the rain sets in. Fog. Bec comes home from school and crawls into a hollow in the middle of the hedge. She comes in at dusk and quietly sets the table as if she's been up in her room or out playing with friends. After Tal swallowed the bottle of Halcyon, Jen and I signed the adoption papers, as if now we three unrhythmed strangers could commit ourselves as one. We added the room we'd been planning for years, in the loft over Jen's horse Damien, thinking it would give Bec some space. But it just kept her separate, kept us all separate.

The snow comes early. On a weekend trip up Rainier we make a bivouac in a small crevasse. The wind howls above us and pulls loose the tarp that we've anchored over our heads. Aardvark grabs a handful of pitons from the bottom of his pack. We rope him in so he won't get blown away while he anchors them into the rock. When we pull him back in his beard is frozen solid; his eyes transfixed, seeming to stare at some unknown point, as if they too might be frozen. We strip off his clothes and zip him into a bag with Bear, who holds him until his body stops vibrating and the color comes back to his lips. When we feel Aardvark's breath return, Buffalo spoons me into his body, his hands wrap around my chest. I sleep.

In the morning we dig ourselves out with our ice axes. Aardvark is in good spirits but his body is worn and tired. He breathes audibly with each movement as if it requires all the oxygen in his body. Thankfully there is color in all of his fingers and toes. The sky clears and slowly we make our way down. Buffalo kicks steps in the snow that would fit two of mine. I slide along behind the others, my toes painfully hitting the fronts of my boots with every step.

We are all so bruised, our skin recently so close to frostbite that it tingles in the crisp morning air. By noon we arrive at the lodge down below, where Aardvark has another name. His wife Emily spots him as we walk in the door and wordlessly pulls him into her body. Her blond curls intertwine with his newly formed black dreadlocks. For a moment they remain still, locked in the embrace that comes only after half a lifetime of intimacy. But then she starts hammering his chest with her small fists.

"You bastard," she screams into his ear, loud enough so we can all hear. "Fucking bastard. What did you want me to tell our babies when they woke up? What? What should I have said?"

He tries to hold her still; his shattered massive down-clad body locks onto her petite frame, but she doesn't stop. She just keeps pounding. The tears come on and on but there are no more words.

Glancing over their heads, I am startled to see Bec asleep on a couch by the fireplace, her head resting on Jen's lap. Emily must have called them when Peter didn't come home. I always tell Jen I'll be away for longer than planned, wanting to avoid any possibility that she'll worry. Jen's eyes find mine through the crowd of reporters and onlookers. I feel the tiredness in her eyes. Her golden-brown hair, usually pulled back tightly into a single braid, now hangs loosely around her face. She hasn't slept.

"Were you frightened?" Suddenly there is a microphone in my face.

I push it away and duck past the reporters to sit on the edge of the couch with Jen and Bec. Taking hold of Jen's hand, I knead her palm with my fingers.

"Sweetie, you're frozen," she says, instinctively pulling back, before reaching around me with her other arm. Feeling Jen shift from underneath her, Bec wakes and wordlessly snuggles up next to me. Like a bear cub, she shoves her head into my middle.

"Were you lost?" she asks. Her voice is so soft I can barely hear her but it is a first—a step toward us. Battered from the trip, I want to be with Jen and Bec—I want Bec to know that I won't leave her. I stay home for three months.

* * *

I remember Tal once told me that Bec loved the potters' wheel. On a whim, I sign us both up for a pottery class at the rec center. Saturday mornings, when I'd normally be driving to the mountains before dawn, Bec and I drive to the market and have coffee by the water before class starts. We sit silently in a café, our legs dangling from our stools. Crumbs from her chocolate croissant fall onto her red high-top canvas sneakers.

After a brief introduction from the teacher, Bec carefully takes the mud-colored clay in her hands and rolls it slowly into a ball before she places it on the wheel. She takes so long to do this that it almost seems as if she's reading the clay. Then she closes her hands around the ball she's created, skillfully molding it into something that was not there before. Sometimes I think she sees something in the clay that none of us do, as if she knows what it wants to be. Our kitchen fills with bowls painted with archaic horses, mugs of various shapes and sizes, and an occasional attempt at a model of a mountain or a horse. Weekday afternoons before Bec gets home, I grade papers, clean the house, and sometimes even make cookies.

"Why are you here?" she asks one day when she stops in the kitchen after school.

"Because you are."

She grabs an oatmeal cookie off the counter and heads out the back door toward her room in the barn.

"Don't knock yourself out," she says, turning back to look at me. "My mom was never around. I can deal."

*   *   *

On a warm day late in the winter I call the school and ask for Bec to be excused for a doctor's appointment.

"What are you doing here?" she asks as she throws her tattered red backpack into the back seat of the Prius. "I don't have a doctor's appointment."

Sometime over the winter she must have started brushing her hair. Bright red in the sunlight, it is now down nearly to her waist.

She's wearing her favorite pair of tattered jeans, the only ones she had when she came.

"There's something we need to do."

I drive to Carkeek Park and pull up almost onto the beach. The only other cars in the acre-size parking lot are a park ranger Jeep and a beat-up red Honda Civic with two teenage boys hanging their heads out the window smoking cigarettes. We both sit silently for a few minutes, staring through the windshield at the water.

"Your mom loved it here." I tell her as we get out of the car.

She turns and looks at me with her big green eyes that seem to take up her whole face. It's the first time I've mentioned my sister since she died.

We pull off our shoes and walk along the beach. The sand is cool and it seeps between our toes as we walk. When we lift our feet, we leave divots that quickly fill with water. Bec stares out across the Sound as if she is looking toward another continent.

"She loved you."

"Right," she murmurs. She turns away and walks back toward the car.

* * *

Spring returns. Walking across the quad to class, I watch the perpetually young—throwing Frisbees, their chests bare and firm, eager for experience. Even the women pull off their t-shirts revealing sports bras of various colors and patterns. The more studious sit in the grass, backs against trees, reading Dante, or trying to solve complicated algebraic formulas. I put a picture taken of us on the summit of Rainier on my otherwise empty desk in my office at school, alongside a picture I took of Bec on the beach at Carkeek, staring out across the water.

The snow pack lets go of its grip on the mountains, turning into liquid as it slides down the rock, into the crevasses, before flowing into the rivers and streams. From there it moves swiftly into the valleys, where it seeps into the soil, hydrating the fields of vegetable crops down below—the same vegetables that Jen and Bec will buy on Sunday mornings later in the summer at Pike Place.

A group of hikers find a woman's body just above eight thousand feet on the Muir Snowfield. She is most likely a member of the Atlanta expedition gone missing since early January. I mourn her loss, a sister climber, as if she were a member of my pack—a woman I met once in a dream.

On weekends, I return to the high country, the naked rock restores my confidence. Our eyes widen, watching a world aired for our presence. We climb the hardest routes like scales. We share high ease, absorb ourselves to rhythmic feet on rock. I'm Lizard, on rock I flow. Sometimes I can't tell where the rock stops and I begin. The dust clears from my brain like mist from the sea. I can see again.

Back in Seattle Jen sits cross-legged sewing colored blankets into a tent. The shack's a roof on space. While Bec is at school, we test it out, tumbling into our living room refuge, laughing uncontrollably until we fall asleep. For a moment I feel like I could live here in the low country. Yet, walking into a store, a bar, I'd think I must have come here by mistake.

Classes end and we bring Jen's tent to Barclay Lake. As soon as we peel off our packs and pitch the tent, Bec runs down a log and jumps fully clothed into the glacier lake. When her body hits the near-frozen water, she squeals and almost flies back to shore before running across the sand and tumbling into our multicolored shack. Jen and I race in after her, and, giggling, bury her beneath mounds of fluffy down sleeping bags. Jen tickles her until she laughs so hard she can barely breathe. We all collapse in a heap. It's only a moment but for a moment I am whole.

We wake to the thundering sound of snow letting go of the summit.

"What is it?" Bec asks.

An avalanche can fall for an hour without making a sound, straight down the mountain wall. I wonder how long we've been sleeping.

"It's a full moon—we might be able to see it." I pull her toward me and unzip the front of the tent. Sure enough, we watch big balls of snow tumble down the mountain and then splash into the far side of the lake. We stay there, our bodies intertwined in the moonlight, listening to the silence punctuated only by the sound of snow crashing into water. Breathing in the sweet spicy fragrance of the white-bark pine trees, I squeeze Bec into my chest. I feel her heart beating. She is so still. So perfect. I wonder how Tal was ever able to leave her.

Jen rubs her eyes to get the sleep out and grabs hold of Bec's shoulder. "And you wonder why the water was cold—well there you have it girlfriend—big huge ice cubes!" Jen laughs.

"How would I know?" Bec squirms around in my arms. She's a little indignant but she's laughing right along with us.

*   *   *

A week later I come home late from a department meeting and wander out to the barn to check on the horses. Jen's old gelding Damien is lying down in his stall, nibbling at a few wisps of hay. And Bec, dressed in her blue-striped pajamas that we gave her for Christmas, is sound asleep next to him, her head resting on his shoulder. Carefully, so as not to disturb Damien, I lift her out of the pine shavings. Thankfully the gelding doesn't move until we are well on our way up to the loft. When I hear him stand up, I stop midway up the stairs and breathe a sigh of relief.

"How long do you think she's been doing that," I ask Jen as I climb into bed.

"A while."

"What do you mean a while, did you think of mentioning this before? He could have rolled on top of her, or stepped on her when he was getting up."

"Sweetie," she rubs her calloused hand along my cheek, "I can't believe you're worried about this. Damien knows she's there—he's not going to hurt her."

I am quiet, not knowing how to answer.

She pulls me close, draws me in. I feel her lips kissing my shoulder and then she too is quiet.

*   *   *

Back in the high country, Buffalo is wearing his red-checked shirt. I wear a scarf to keep my hair in place. We struggle to hold on but the wind blows us apart. Three on a rope, threading a bridge of snow. We pull at one another, can't seem to find the way to commit. I shove my canteen down into the stream, letting water trickle over the lip. Yesterday they said, a man fell in, was buried under snow and left, just like that, by his friends for dead. Sleeping on the ledge, I move away from the others. In the morning, I coil my rope and walk away. I want to be home by dark.

Pulling into the driveway I see Jen in the field on Diamond, the dark bay four-year-old she bought last spring at auction. He seems to bounce more than walk as he moves his body effortlessly across the field. It's a mystery to me how Jen stays on him. The danger so inherent, so close. I've seen him leap into the air on all four legs, like a cat, before returning to the earth where the rest of us mortals reside. He never loses a beat, sometimes even continuing to canter in midair with all four feet off the ground. I stop the engine and quietly open my door before realizing that they are not alone. Silhouetted behind Jen and Diamond, Bec sits on Damien. From a distance, I can barely tell them apart, two dark bay horses, completely in stride. As I watch them canter across the field, Bec and Jen's hair blows loose behind them in the faint wind, making a cloud around their faces that seems to glimmer in the quiet still light of dusk. I feel as though I'm looking at a painting. For a moment I think I have double vision—I rub my hands over my eyes because I can't separate the two horses. The still center's a paradox. That's it. That's motion in its place.

RACHEL MARKELS WEBBER *spent much of her childhood in Seattle, Washington and Boulder, Colorado. The*

daughter of mountain climbers, she spent many weekends hiking with her parents. Rachel currently lives in Massachusetts where she trains Dressage Horses and their riders. "Above Snowline" is her second published short story; her first, "Missing"
appeared in the Charles River Review.

Mortal Champions

Stefani Nellen

At a small track meet in college, many years ago, I had what might be called a near-death experience. Based on the few things I heard from those who saw it happen, I have to conclude that it probably looked pretty embarrassing from the outside.

Here is what I remember: I ran the mile, the slower of two heats. At the time, I read Bannister's autobiography, about how he would run in a park at night without keeping track of time, chasing and inhaling his own breath. I fantasized about the heat between his tracksuit and his skin. Something turned: I wanted him (and judging from his autobiography his younger self might have been too humble, awkward, and polite to refuse me)—then I wanted *it*, the thing I saw in him—then I wanted to *be* it, and then I was doomed.

We lined up for the race. The guy next to me angled his torso forward. His last name was Connor. Right away, he took the lead and hammered away. A group rallied to give chase, and I was among them. At halfway, Connor was still ahead and looked to stay there. We were satisfied keeping an eye on him, expecting him to crash and fall back. Our coach called out to me: "Relax, for God's sake." I felt like shit, my intestines wanted to burst out of me, and my breath was wet and pleading, like a bad porn soundtrack. It was now Peter van Meer, George Howe, and I giving chase, and Connor looked over his shoulder. His face was burning. Spit hung from his chin.

The official leaned forward to change the marker to one lap to go. He started to turn the leaf when Connor passed him and was done when we ran past; he was an old guy who took his task seriously. The wind blew up his white hair, and with the breeze came a foolish hope. I accelerated. My stomach turned into acid, and the audience cheered. Peter and George immediately covered my move and overtook me, the crowd cheered again, and before I knew it I was chasing Peter and George, who were chasing Connor. I lost contact. I had one move left and pulled up even with George's right elbow, and they ditched me again, this time for good. The chase pack overtook me, a whole train of them, like the band of demigods in the opening sequence of *Chariots of Fire*. Someone in the stands distributed ice cream cones from a freezer bag. I wanted one. I was running last.

Connor went all out on the final straight, and everyone screamed in a frenzy. My legs became numb, and then I couldn't feel them at all. My ankle crunched, a crack from deep inside my ears. I fell forward, tried to catch myself with my arms, and found they had gone, replaced by appendages that flailed like a pet monkey's. My face hit the track. Blood and rubber exploded in my mouth as I rolled across the lanes. All movement ceased.

The others ran on, unaware of my fall, and even if they had known they'd have been unwilling to sacrifice the race so close to the finish. My world became a segment of track, my horizon the crumbling delimiter of the infield and the tips of grass behind it.

When it was over, someone turned me on my back. The coach leaned over me and flung words at me I didn't recognize. Like fish food in a bowl, the sounds drifted toward each other and struggled to cohere. He pincered my eyelids with thumb and forefinger and hitched them up and down. My vision blurred and cleared. He brought his ear close to my lips, pressed his hand on my chest.

My eyes burned, unblinking. Hot spit ran from the corner of my mouth. I couldn't wipe it off, couldn't even flick my tongue. More liquid welled out; my body convulsed—a slow wave from torso to feet, nerve signals originating from not-me—and I squirmed out of the grip of paralysis to puke. My eyes closed, finally. Pain roared in and settled on the side of my face and in the roots of my front teeth.

Then, I plain felt like shit. This, I could deal with.

I sat up, tested my limbs, and tried to act like someone who wakes up with a nasty hangover. I grimaced and groaned.

"You gave us a good scare," our coach said.

"You're welcome."

Connor kicked my foot and said, *I'm glad you're okay, man*, but he really meant, *thanks for stealing my thunder, wimp.*

Later, the team doctor referred to the incident as a "case of nerves." The story was that I went out way too fast and dealt with my panic and skyrocketing oxygen debt by falling on my face. "It's more common with girls," he said. Shortly after, I quit the team. No one pressed me for the reasons. I didn't feel I could live down the spectacle of my "nerves" or come out about the low-tier fan fiction of my Bannister fantasies. I researched diseases that started with falls like mine, and found many: a library of horror stories all potentially my own.

I couldn't do without running, of course, and a few years later I started jogging again. My body remembered the "fit," like pain from a broken bone that flares up in bad weather. I knew I wouldn't be done with this until I stepped on a track again for another race. When I was in my forties, it was time.

*   *   *

By then, I had taken over a snake's nest of a psychology department as an outside head. My job was to siphon the energy previously spent on inter-lab warfare into actual research. Every morning, I met my two running buddies, Rick and Fabrice, at a nearby trailhead, and we'd take off for a run in the park. I'd met them the morning Barry and I moved into our house on Carnegie Place.

But before I laid eyes on either of them, I met Rick's wife, Felina. She reprimanded our movers for blocking her driveway.

"Imagine," she said. "My husband is out on a run, and he's hit by a car. I need to get to him as fast as I can, but my car is blocked. Because of this." She pointed at the moving van. "*Ryan Moving and Storage*," she read from the van's side. "That's what I'll tell myself for the rest of my life. I couldn't be with him when he needed me, because of Ryan Moving and Storage."

She spoke calmly, her gaze boring into mine. She appeared so convinced of the danger looming above her husband that I felt it, too—as if, by leaving the van where it was, I'd be responsible for the inevitable car crash and everything that followed.

Just when I was about to offer my apologies, two runners rounded the corner, a tall man and a small one. Felina exhaled and closed her eyes. I was relieved, too. I felt a minor but profound shift inside me, as if my life had for a moment been on the brink of disaster and fallen back on the safe side.

One of the runners, the man I'd later know as Rick Ricci—Felina's husband—was clearly a former track runner. You could tell it by his stride, by his muscular legs that carried the afterthought of his barrel-chested torso, and by he way he planted his feet toes first. But his past on the track would have been obvious to me even if he'd been old and overweight and wearing a tweed suit. There's something about the mindless grace of offering hundreds of miles to the great unknown that other runners recognize immediately.

Fabrice was one of us, too: small, with a beer belly and a mop of sweaty brown hair. Before shaking my hand, he wiped his on a checkered bandana that dangled from the waistband of his baseball shorts.

By now, Barry had joined us. "We moved to Fit Street, I see."

"I'd call it Faded Glory Boulevard," Rick said.

"Our fast runs used to be our slow runs," Fabrice said.

"You can say that again," I said.

"Tragic," Barry said. "What a collection of has-beens."

"Just saying it like it is," Fabrice said.

"So you all used to run in college?" Barry asked.

"Yes," we three runners said, and laughed.

"Why don't we run together," I added on a whim. "I could use the accountability."

"Right on," Rick said. "Bright and early. Six a.m. tomorrow."

* * *

The trail we took led right down into a gorge. When we emerged again, sweaty and hurting and damn proud of it, Felina sat in her car at the corner of Reynolds and Carnegie, waiting for us with her window rolled down. Rick waved at her across the lawn and she waved back and took off. She was the breadwinner, working a corporate job downtown. I was curious about the morning ritual and the reason for their division of labor—if there was a reason—but I didn't want to pry. Running was our neutral territory. We needed a place where we could be almost anonymous: a three-man army uniformed in moisture-wicking fabrics and shock-absorbent shoes that gave us a smooth ride. I'd hear the truth soon enough.

* * *

"Ready?" Rick said, and as always Fabrice and I said, "No," and we took off. We took the steepest route down in order to pick up gravity-assisted speed, but the level trail at the bottom never failed to kill the illusion. Fabrice was usually the first to lose form, but he never caved; he stuck to the pace better than I could, and this morning was no exception. When we reached the clearing with the water fountain and the apple green doggy bowl—the farthest point of our run—it was I who asked for a break.

Rick glared at his watch, and then at me. He made a sweeping gesture at our surroundings: the trail behind us, the abandoned picnic table, the freeway in the distance. "This isn't cutting it anymore." He grabbed my upper arm and pulled at it, pulled me closer to him. He'd never touched me before. "Come on. You used to run track. Three, four miles through the park, at a snail's pace? Don't tell me it doesn't pain you."

Fabrice was done drinking at the water fountain and joined us. His shirt stuck to his wet chest.

"What we need," Rick said, "is a proper race. A race on a track. A race we can train for."

"I vote for something short," Fabrice said.

"The mile," Rick said.

"Sounds good." Fabrice pulled his bandana from his waistband and wiped his face and shoulders. "What? Everyone can suck it up for one mile."

*　*　*

Rick and Felina invited us over to their place for the first time. It was a muggy, dark day. We sat at a table in the backyard. Fabrice was already there when we arrived. He and Rick had known each other forever; they'd grown up in each other's houses, but I hadn't noticed their familiarity with each other before, and how it excluded me. On the trail, running made us equals.

We talked logistics about the race. "If it's a track mile, it will be a small affair," Felina said. "You'll have space for, what, ten competitors? Fifteen?"

"That doesn't have to be a problem," said Barry. "You could have seeded races, go from slowest to fastest. I can help keep track of the qualifiers."

"Sorry, but this sounds too complicated," said Felina. "Why not make it one big event for everyone? Like a road 5K. People pay to enter, and the money goes to a neighborhood project. Say, Celine's dog shelter or something."

"I don't know, guys," Fabrice said. "I like the idea of running on a track. It has class."

It occurred to me that Fabrice might beat me. Some people are born fast and don't feel pain the way others do.

"Why not both?" Barry said. "Start out with the mile, and then run the 5K. The 5K runners warm up by cheering you milers."

"Do we even know how to do this?" I said. "We need timing mats, we need permits, and we need a measured course . . ."

"I know people who organize local races each year," Rick said. "It won't be a problem." I believed him. I'd looked him up online, of course, and seen that as recently as two years ago, he'd made the podium at some of these local races he'd mentioned: the Firecracker 5K, the Gutbuster.

"I talked to a few running clubs, too," he said. "They're going to spread the word. I won't be just the three of us lining up."

"They'd do anything for you," Felina said.

'They'd do anything to promote the sport," he said.

"Uh huh," she said. "That's why they'll run some obscure track mile when you ask them to. Because they love the sport."

An uncomfortable silence settled on us.

"Maybe we should tell them," Felina said to Rick.

Fabrice raised his hand. "I vote in favor."

"Rick?"

"All right."

Felina crossed her legs and gathered herself. She leaned forward. "Two years ago, Rick was abducted." She glanced at him. "If that is what happened. We're still not sure. It started out as this classic scenario. Husband goes out for a run and doesn't come back."

"Honey."

She turned in her chair to address him as well as us. I got the sense she wanted to see the effect each of her sentences had on him. She was treading carefully. "A week later, they found you walking along the interstate, completely out of it. You had a head wound. At first you weren't talking. After a month, you did. But your voice had changed. It never changed back."

"It's wild," he said lamely. "When you watch old movies of me or something, it's like listening to a different person."

"Except you're not different," she said. "You remember who you are. You remember now."

He nodded obediently. "I do remember."

"So that's where we're at," Felina said, still talking more to Rick than to us. "You're a survivor. Of course they'll want to celebrate you by running a mile. The question is do you want to go back there. Do you want this attention now."

"I just want to go out there and kick ass."

*　*　*

"So what do you think?" Barry said when we were back home on our porch.

"About Rick? I think he needs this."

"Like a form of therapy?"

"Yes, but without the talking." I massaged my leg.

"So he never mentioned any of this to you."

"No. If we talk, we only talk about running." My leg felt weird. Itchy and numb at the same time. "I think I feel it again. That tingle I sometimes have."

"You mean like ants crawling up and down?"

"Yes. I almost fell again this morning."

"It's a bumpy trail."

"No. This was different."

The houses in our street looked more similar to each other in the dark than they did at daylight. A few houses down, Rick wandered about in his living room, already in his running clothes, picking up things.

"He's training on his own," I said. "I saw him a few times. He's getting fast."

"I told you before, if you're really worried about what's happening to your legs, or your nerves, or whatever your current theory is—"

"I know I sound ridiculous—"

"No, my point is: go see a doctor, and have it checked out. Don't put on your running shoes and break your back stumbling over a tree root."

"Roger Bannister used to run at night."

Barry took hold of my shoulders. "Roger Bannister was a doctor."

We kissed. The Ricci screen door creaked open and fell shut, and Rick's steps pattered down the street.

*   *   *

The Riccis decided to go along with the plan of running two races: first a mile on the track, then a 5K fun run for all comers. The 5K start and finish would be at a parking lot next to the track. The course was already certified for the Race for the Cure. Miller's Bakery became our biggest sponsor, and the three of us started to refer to our race as The Jelly Doughnut Mile.

Fun stopped, however, as soon as we set foot on the track. Gone were the mornings of running through the park and pretending to be three middle-aged guys who wanted to stay in shape. We were in serious training now. We did quarters, two hundreds, three hundreds, quarters, eight hundreds, quarters, three hundreds, and all out two hundreds. Rick timed us. We felt he should; he was our leader in this, the one with the stakes.

A locker-room building stood on one side of the track, a picnic table at the other. I used these two markers to pace myself through the workouts. At times, my mind drifted and I was watching the three of us from above, clicking off speed and rest intervals like clockwork, each taking his turn in front.

"It's going to be a strong field," Rick panted as we steamed off between sets. "The Duquesne team is in." They were a college team. Their best runner held the state steeplechase record. Rick had also invited a couple of strong masters runners with PRs faster than mine, and he and Fabrice would definitely dust me on race day. My only shot at not finishing last in the Jelly Doughnut Mile now rested with someone else screwing up. Maybe I would, again.

I rolled my toes inside my spikes and shook out my legs, feeling for the familiar numbness. Sometimes it was there, sometimes it wasn't. Usually it was, but I managed to block it out. The beep of Rick's watch announced the next interval. Fabrice sprinted to the front with ease.

* * *

Felina ran towards me in the park. It was late, almost dark.

I wasn't running, just walking, trying to clear my head two days out from race day. My leg symptoms were nearly constant now. I had to pay attention to how I planted my foot. What did it mean? I'd dialed my doctor's number a few times, and hung up before anyone took the call. I had to run the mile first. I had to run it without falling down. Most people wouldn't get it, but a few would, and they'd be enough.

Felina was with me now, out of breath. "Have you seen Rick?"

I had, on Tranquil Trail. I told her, and that I'd been surprised to see him up there. We were supposed to rest up.

She bristled. "He's been running for hours every day. He's killing himself."

"Did you try to talk to him?"

She waved away the possibility. "He can't come last at the race," she then said. "It would destroy him."

"I don't think he'll be last."

"Good." She rubbed her arms. "But can't you make sure?"

"You mean I should let him beat me?"

"Yes."

"As I said, I don't think it will be necessary to pretend. He's in excellent shape."

"So your answer is no. I could have guessed."

"I just don't think it would help."

"You don't know him the way I do."

I couldn't argue with that.

"I'll try Fabrice," she said.

*　　*　　*

Race Day. The track was swarming with people, mostly runners and spectators of the 5K that would start after the mile. People drove around searching for parking spaces, families spread out picnic blankets, and the air smelled of sunscreen and doughnuts and coffee. The timing guys sat huddled over computers next to the timing mat at the 5K start that would also be its finish line. Music blasted from the speakers, an upbeat rock number I couldn't place.

Rick and I nodded at each other across the infield. My body felt light around me. The mesh of my racing flats tickled my feet. My doctor's appointment was next week. The music faded to the background, and an announcer came on. "All right. Everyone head on up to the track for the mile race, we're about to get started!"

Rick took off his gray shirt and handed it to Felina, who gathered it in front of her belly. He wore red shorts and singlet, and cobalt-blue spikes.

"Oh shit," I said to Barry. "He's open for business."

The Duquesne team warmed up on the track, young and bare chested and reptilian. At the center of the infield, a man in a Pikes Peak Marathon shirt ate a sandwich while rotating his pelvis. Barry was off to buy doughnuts for a late breakfast.

I walked up to Rick. "How are you?"

"I'm all right. You?" His guard was up and solid. He hated my pity, accepted it as inevitable, a nuisance.

"Never been better."

A group of kids crossed the track, chasing each other and blowing soap bubbles.

"Not quite the Olympics," I said.

"A race is a race." He looked at me, testing whether we were on the same page. And we were.

"Mile runners to the start!"

We lined up: Rick, Pikes Peak, Fabrice, a tall guy named Steve and a short guy named Steve, a couple of others, and I. Of course, there was also the Duquesne team. They smelled of algae. Maybe they had a lucky deodorant. The music stopped. The line of people around the track was closing. An official lifted the starting gun.

"On your marks."

My core temperature dropped as a hush fell over us. We took a step forward and froze.

"Set."

I missed the gun and followed the others in a panic. The Duquesne boys moved in another dimension and glided away from us. I managed to latch on to Pikes Peak. After one lap, I found my rhythm and overtook him. Team Duquesne hadn't lapped me yet, and everyone around the track was cheering. I was running next to short Steve. He tried to shake me, but I went with him. Idiot, I told myself, don't start racing yet. But I did.

At the half mile, Rick was about two hundred yards ahead of me. With a burst of insanity, I went after him. He started to turn his head; I knew he'd heard me. I worried him. I scared him. I had him.

Ahead of Rick, Fabrice and tall Steve were neck and neck. Rick and I were flotsam in their wake. This flare of insight—that we were competing for eighth versus ninth place—burned away what little caution I had. I hit the accelerator.

The leaders went into the final bend. The cheers grew louder, tense, agonized.

Rick stuck with me. Good job, I thought, but not good enough, sucker. Short Steve caught a second wind and overtook us. He ran like a schoolboy who missed the bus. I hurt badly and so, judging from his groans, did Rick. He pulled even with me again, I went wide to keep him from passing, and far ahead of us someone younger and better won the race.

The announcer started yelling, the spectators screamed, and amidst it all, Rick managed to turn to me the exact moment I turned to him. His eyes were mad, his teeth too white. After an eternity, the final straight rolled out before us. We sprinted. The finish line jerked away from us with each step. Rick was next to me, still. Die, I thought. Die already. We were two banged-up race cars sliding towards the finish, parts coming off and going up in flames. Cheers rose—for us this time. And as we dove for the finish, I had more than Rick. Just a little more inside these legs that quit on me once.

* * *

The final steps are a blur. We dive across the line, and at first it's a replay of my fall years ago: my body spins and crashes, I bounce and roll across the track, skin tears from my hands and knees. It's done; the eagle has landed. Lying on my back, I bring my hands to my face, and taste salt and metal. My heart presses blood into the stiffening pools of skinless flesh at my knees and palms, surge after surge of neutral pressure— until the alarm blares: we have pain, like hooks lifting my flesh in the places where the skin is missing.

Fabrice walks up to me, throws his rag on my face, and I wipe myself off as best as I can. Slowly, I get up.

Rick is still down, on his side, his back to me. Felina is squatting next to him, her lips moving. She swivels her head, gets up, and hurries off with a frown.

"Good run," says Fabrice.

"You too."

Attention wanes: the 5K start is in ten minutes. Farther off, Barry is leaning against the fence and shaking his head, a bag of doughnuts in his hand. I want to stagger towards him and embarrass him with a bloody kiss on the lawn.

But first: Rick. He's still on his side with his back to us, so Fabrice and I walk around him. His eyes are wide open, his arms stretched out in front of him. He is focusing on his fingers. I kick his foot with mine in a gesture that could have meant, "way to steal my thunder, wimp," and that really means, "I'm glad you're okay."

Is he okay? I offer my hand, brace myself for the pain his touch will bring, and after a moment he takes it and sits up. Felina approaches with a medic, and Rick gestures at me and says, "Check him out first, I'm okay."

Fabrice says, "I could murder a doughnut." I point at Barry. Fabrice limps towards him with sounds of gladness. As the medic disinfects my hands, cranking up the volume of my pain for a few hot seconds, Rick and I look at each other.

"Good job," he says. "Nice rust buster. Next time, it's mine. Hey, Fabrice!"

"That's the spirit," I say. The medic proceeds to my knees and shoots liquid fire into the gashes there. "That's the spirit!" I call out. Blood is oozing down my shins and my legs hurt like hell.

STEFANI NELLEN *is a German psychologist with an MFA in Creative Writing from the Bennington Writing Seminars. Her stories appear in* Guernica, AGNI, Glimmer Train, Third Coast, Bellevue Literary Review, PRISM International, *and* Cutbank, *among others. She is also a graduate of the Clarion Science Fiction and Fantasy Workshop. Her real home is currently in the Netherlands with her family; her online home is at stefaninellen.com.*

———————

Everyday Horror Show

Paola Ferrante

I t starts as mostly nothing, just the wind. You want to have a baby, and when she's born it's the middle of the afternoon, not even dark and stormy, even if smog covers the sun. You want to hold your baby; you take her home in your arms to a second-floor apartment in an old Victorian. You hold your baby, you feed your baby; any noise in the attic is just a rattling pipe, or a squirrel that's been chased from its backyard home by your terrier, or the process of settling. (In a haunting, leave out the part where you're afraid. It's easy to mistake the sound of wind for ghosts, or the sound of fear; run a windbreaker over the tire of a wheelbarrow, place the arm of a record player on a towel, touch the needle to the cloth, tap lightly to make a low-end thump. Tap faster. Tap faster. No one else will see it. They will say it's just your heart.)

Of course you want to hold your baby, but there are cold spots, mysterious drafts in the baby's room. There is an unexplained chill that keeps you up past early morning feedings; there's never any time to take a shower before the water becomes something between January slush and summer hail. There is the space heater that you set, every single day, on *High Heat Mode*, which keeps switching back to *Natural Wind*. It knocks over the vase of roses on your

109

daughter's nightstand, and it's not like you want to worry, but the buds from the overturned bouquet bother you. They remind you of fruit trees that should be in bloom; the instructor at the class for expecting parents who liked to compare the size of the baby to fruits. At nine weeks, baby was a cherry, at thirteen, a peach. At fourteen weeks baby was a lemon; you didn't tell your husband about watching *The Blue Planet*, that for now, even if lemons might be one of the only things predicted to survive in the event of a global climate catastrophe, they wouldn't survive if temperatures rose more than two degrees. He wouldn't see the point, even though he is the one who has already started looking at universities. It hasn't happened yet. Why worry about what isn't right in front of you? You want to want to hold your baby, but when you try to rock your daughter back to sleep in her cozy fleece, something always runs an icy sliver through your shoulder. (Leave out the part where you check for drafts, searching for candles in boxes labelled *Attic, Fragile, Handle with Care,* and something invisible spells along your arm in goosebumps, a cold braille that reads *Get out,* or maybe *Help?*) When you rest her head on your shoulder your baby cries. Your baby always cries, and frost forms on the outer petals in your bouquet of rose buds with its big pink congratulations.

Your husband says you should check the thermostat. Your husband says, *Did you close the windows?* Your husband says, *I don't know what you want. It's an old house.* His voice on the phone from Texas is distant, like your best friend from college who calls while she's working on another B-movie horror film, tells you that you're lucky you got what you wanted when you're changing diapers and you can't begin to tell her how you miss being covered in fake bodily fluids. You could just be exaggerating. *After all, you always say you're cold,* your husband says. You know he's thinking about your thirty-seventh birthday in the summer, the one where you were both on that set of a *Blair Witch* soft remake that used snow made of pig fat to mimic a winter's night. He was the best boy; you slipped and slid in pig fat in the middle of a heat wave for fourteen hours a day, trying to set up the mics until you were covered in it, until he talked about holding your future daughter while strangers pinched her chunky cheeks, until you told him you just wanted things to change before it was too late. Later, when you both told the crew you were getting married, the card said congratulations with two skeleton buzzards, one groom, one bride on the front with a stroller. Despite the fact that sixty-six people had already died of the heat wave in Montreal, you had to borrow his sweater. *Maybe it's just you.* Of course he can't just come home. Of course all this is what you wanted. (You want to want your baby, but she won't stop crying, and your breath and hers fog up and freeze together in tiny fractals on the window in the middle of July.)

*   *   *

Then the wailing starts. Every night there's wailing, but what did you expect? It's not a hungry cry, or a tired cry, or a gassy cry, or a cuddle cry. It might be a scared cry, some otherworldly weeping, along with the occasional blood-curdling scream while your terrier barks along all night. Your mother-in-law says it's expected. Your mother-in-law says it's colic; *Lots of babies have colic under four months old,* she says when she sits down with a cup of coffee at your kitchen table. *I'm sure if your mother was still around, she would say the same.* It's expected. (Even if, when no one should be up at this hour, there is the sound of disembodied footsteps to the kitchen. It could be boots knocking against the heater; even if the footsteps are accompanied by weeping after your baby is finally asleep and it pours inside the bathroom, it could be your mother-in-law prepping breakfast, the sound of frying bacon for rain.) It's nothing to be concerned about if you've already seen the pediatrician; *What did you expect? When I had mine, there was crying for twenty-three hours a day, seven days a week.* Haven't you taken your daughter out for a ride in the car or the stroller? Haven't you used white noise; haven't you tried doing a load of laundry, maybe running the vacuum once in a while? When you get up to get your coffee your mother-in-law puts her hand over the sugar bowl you are trying to refill. *Have you tried cutting out sugar and coffee and chocolate?* Yes, even chocolate, even if you read how all the cocoa plants in Africa will soon be gone. Of course you haven't, so your daughter will keep crying; what's happening is what your mother-in-law expected. (And what did you expect, having your mother-in-law stay with you to help, when you can't explain why sometimes, when you go to the bathroom in the middle of the night, there's so much weeping it's raining from the ceiling. Like in the haunting where the Gardners found water dripping from their walls in the middle of drought, you're not sure if it's tears or your breasts that have leaked through the towel you wrapped around yourself to sleep in.) You dump your coffee in the sink. Of course you only want what's best for your daughter; your best is what's expected. You put salt instead of sugar in your mother-in-law's cup. You're not sure where you put your sugar; you must just be tired. Of course you're tired. What did you expect?

*   *   *

The mothers in the group say, *It's milk brain. You should try not to worry.* The mothers are all spread out on blankets in the park, and you are sitting on your only clean towel. The mothers in the group your downstairs neighbor with the two three-year-old boys recommended *because you have to get out of this place sometime* say, *Try to enjoy being in a gooshy love bubble.* The mothers all have names, but mostly they are you. (At least they're how you know you should try to be.) There is the you who's self-settling, but still sleeping, somehow able to ignore the wailing through her house at night, the you who needs to be shown how to use a woven wrap as a transitional womb but never says she's worried about invisible fingers untying the ends, the you who only feeds her kid organics but never talks about how when it comes to beets, her bathroom turns the color of the elevator in *The Shining. You should try making your own baby food; you'll notice the difference. You should use a ring sling instead, they're easier for beginners.* You try to smile. You pass the sugar cookies.

When the circle comes around to the you, you say your daughter keeps crying and spitting up when you feed her, and no one even mentions Linda Blair. *You should try baby-wearing to soothe her; you should try rainfall white-noise playlists. Acid reflux is pretty normal in babies under six months. You should try not to worry.* The mothers all speak as one, like those images of bees before a colony collapses. You want to ask, but aren't you scared of a cold, intentional wind loosening a ring sling, that if you make sounds of rain around your daughter they will flood you both, create a monsoon from the ceiling? You want to ask, but your daughter spits up and you realize you forgot your baby bag. (You should try being more prepared; it's easy to mistake a record player for your thumping heartbeat, a microphone in your mouth which gives a low-end sound for the blood rushing faster through your veins. No one would believe like in the case of the Zugun poltergeist girl, invisible hands moved your baby bag to somewhere between worlds; if you try to hunt for wipes in your purse, no one would believe a ghost put a bottle of wine in there, especially when you're breastfeeding.) You should go. *You should try to enjoy your time with her; it goes so fast.* The mother sitting on the blanket beside you says you should stay until the end; she'll help you find the wipes. She says your daughter will be fine, but you can't explain how when you look at your daughter with spit up all over her polar bear bib you feel a paranormal disconnect, like she is some other species who can't survive with you like this; you can't explain how your heart thumping is mistaken for a record player but is really just a panic. You can't explain why a bottle of wine, dumped out on the beach towel beside your keys, is in your purse. (And what kind of mother tries to go sleep by keeping wine in her purse; what kind of mother has a daughter when she worries that soon all the grapes in the world will be gone? What kind of mother has a daughter when she knows she has a ghost?) Before she saw the bottle, the mother beside you said; *Things like this happen all the time. Try not to think of it as the end of the world.* There wasn't room, beside her still nearly-full Tupperware of sugar cookies, to say you were scared it might be.

*   *   *

Your husband doesn't see it. You're trying not to think of ghosts, but your terrier has begun to dig herself a hole in the background where you find the torn-out blank pages of your daughter's baby book, some action figures that you know are made from nonrecyclable plastic that belong to your downstairs neighbor's sons. You're trying on the rare nights your mother-in-law goes home and you and your husband are both home and in bed together and he says, *See, now this is just like our first date.* That afternoon the extras snuck a case of beer on set and the two of you grabbed a few and got drunk doing improv in the park. He laid down behind you and you asked if he was impersonating a spoon. Afterward, you took the subway and there was that woman, with nothing in her stroller but packets of seeds. So you gave her one of the beers; you couldn't stop laughing. *Do you remember?* You're trying, but you want to tell him you can't stop seeing what isn't there; there's nothing on the baby book pages for baby's first smile and laugh. Instead you find newspaper clippings about wildfires or floods around the house; he says why don't you try not worrying? Can you focus on the positive? You're trying. You try to remember how when you attempted to grow violets from the woman's seeds, he said, *Let's make a baby instead.* (To make a sound that's easily mistaken for arousal, or blood rushing in your veins, put your mouth around that mike, or use the sound of a sponge you squeezed into water.) When your husband presses up against your back, a little voice inside you thinks *light as a feather, stiff as a board* and you tense and roll away.

You're trying. Your husband doesn't see it. In the morning, the spoons inside the kitchen drawers are always gone.

*   *   *

You say you're trying, but your mother-in-law doesn't see it. You watch her play with your daughter with the plastic turtle that she got her, the same one you thought about buying but then worried that when she was old enough, your daughter would have no idea what it was, just like the beanie baby dodo bird you lost when you were a kid. (You're trying, but you can't stop thinking about the South Shields haunting, where the mother was attacked by her child's plastic dog, which flew across the room, where she fought a bunny with a box cutter at the top of the stairs.) When your daughter plays with your mother-in-law who calls her *my dear,* your daughter smiles and coos the way she doesn't with you. (You tried once to make the sound of a baby cooing by recording pigeons, but no one could mistake that sound.) Your mother-in-law says try not to worry, but after your daughter is asleep, you watch the images of turtles eating plastic bags and all you see in the blue light of the screen is that they look like ghosts. You're trying to pack your daughter's diaper bag so you can both can go to the park together to go to mommy-and-me yoga, but the fog descends from the ceiling and you're always missing something, a blanket, ten or so wipes in a plastic bag, at least one diaper, a container of hand sanitizer, more plastic bags for your daughter's dirty diapers, even if they are killing the whales. When you have to buy more bags at the store before you can go to the park you can't remember the word biodegradable and your mother-in-law has already put plastic garbage bags in your cart; the sixteen-year-old can't understand over the soundtrack of your crying child while you scream at your mother-in-law, say you wanted the ones that didn't become what turtles could think were jellyfish.

Your mother-in-law tells your husband you're not even trying to make this work while he's still in LA. The night she leaves you see your downstairs neighbor hanging Christmas lights on the main floor windows of the old Victorian. Your hands are full of soon-to-be jellyfish as you're trying to get your crying daughter back to sleep by taking her for a ride in the car.

I've been meaning to ask how you're doing, your neighbor says and you try to say you're fine; you don't expect to see your neighbor. You don't expect to see Christmas lights in August; she says, *I know it's early, but you know how it is. The darkness in this place can really get to you.* You might be trying not to cry, but you notice the lights are every color but blue; what is left of the blue lights are ragged edges of glass in their sockets.

What happened to the blue ones? you ask.

No idea. She laughs. You're tired, but you can think of all the horror-show possibilities; a vengeful ghost sending a warning, a weirdo living in the basement, the one who smashes them as a message, a confused, exhausted songbird who sees minisuns and, singing all day, forgets to find food for the nest, a child eating what he thinks are blueberries before the trip to the emergency room. *You know, your daughter's eyes are really blue,* your neighbor says, *but they probably won't stay that color. Same thing happened with my sons.*

As she plugs in the light string with all the missing sockets, you ask her, *Aren't you worried?*

All the time. Don't get me wrong, she says, *there was a time when I would have driven on thirty minutes of sleep with both my boys in the back seat to every twenty-four-hour Walmart just to test replacement bulbs in every socket to make sure everything was perfect.* As you stand there talking, you can feel one of the plastic bags slip out from your fingers. Your daughter watches it, stops crying. You watch, defeated, as it dances its way across the lawn, is blown by the wind quite possibly far enough to go into the ocean down in a predictable ghostly blob. *You just have to learn to let some things go.*

When she puts up the lights, your neighbor doesn't bother to staple the last string in the middle. She hangs it instead, in an upside-down rainbow, one that looks tired, one which still is not a smile, even if it looks like one from far away.

*   *   *

You're tired, but you take your screaming daughter out for a ride in the car at night, end up past the end of the block, past the suburbs, where there's forest going up the mountain before she's finally quiet. It's easy to mistake the lulling sound of a car ride when your eyes have almost closed. For driving on gravel you can use the sound of a plastic bag; this also works for driving in the rain. It's easy, when you look quickly, to mistake a woman or a

girl with her thumb extended outward for absolutely nothing;
the corners of your eyes are easily misled, especially late at night,
especially when you're tired. Of course you're tired. You're always
tired. You won't know what you were thinking, driving tired with
your baby. If something happened it would be terrible. (It would
explain how you feel.)

You're tired, and your daughter's still crying, and it's starting
to rain so you stop the car, roll down the window in the rain. You
think maybe, if you and your daughter listen long enough, there
will be just enough rain for sleep. You're tired so you don't really
hear a woman's footsteps in the woods near the tree line, slowly
exiting the woods; they could have been a deer's, you could have
put new aluminum foil on a pillow, covered it with a thin cotton
sheet, then pushed on the surface using your hands to mimic steps.
No one will believe you heard a weeping woman, in a dripping
thin wet dress, asking you to get her out of here. You could have
learned to imitate the sound of a water droplet hitting a lake using
only your mouth and hands. Wet your lips. Drink a glass or two of
water or apply lip balm. Even if you can't whistle, you can pucker
your lips slightly with a gap between them for air to pass through,
then tap the outside of your cheek with a finger, the same as how
when you were a girl you crossed your fingers behind your back, the
opposite of pinky swear. (Leave out the part where you pull over.
Leave out the part where you pick up a hitchhiker, even with your
baby in the back seat of the car and you drive, faster and faster, as
the weeping woman sits silently.) Your daughter is asleep, the soft
spot on the top of her head is hidden by a hat you didn't know to
knit, but your mother-in-law did. The soft spot bothers you. It is
only as strong as that half a watermelon you kept in the fridge for
a month. (Last week, you watched the watermelon hover on the
counter like Humpty Dumpty playing chicken while your daughter
screamed from the living room before it hurled itself over the edge,
creating a morbidly satisfying red splatter.) You didn't mean to let
it go bad; it was an accident. (Leave out the part where there's an
accident. Leave out the part where the woman in your car says

she hasn't been the same since her accident. It's easy to mistake a sheet of metal and balloon dragged across a carpet tile to make a controllable squealing sound for your car swerving when you see a deer; leave out the part where you start thinking of those old crash test dummy commercials, the ones where mommy dummy is tired, mommy dummy isn't watching, mommy dummy didn't put baby in an approved car seat. It's easy to mistake the sound of a sledgehammer in a junkyard for the tree you hit with your car as you swerved to avoid a deer that came out of nowhere; at the moment of impact, baby is a watermelon, smashed on the ground.) You check the rear-view mirror. You get out of the chair to check the back seat; your daughter is still sleeping soundly. (When you looked in the rear-view mirror the woman had vanished, leaving a small imprint of wet on your upholstery. You can't tell anyone. No one would believe you. Leave out the part where the woman may have been dead already. There was some stiffness from rigor mortis in her legs, but she still kicked the dirt off her feet politely before closing the back door.)

*   *   *

The doctor says you're fine; it's nothing. Just a fender-bender. Of course, your daughter's fine. You're tired, but you have to agree you're fine. Yes, you're fine, but you're not sleeping. But that's considered pretty normal. (Anyone would have trouble sleeping; in your house the stairs creak, and the doors bang and the TV turns on like the radio in the Thornton Heath haunting, you'd swear by itself, so you end up watching how bees are dying all the fruit in the world will be gone.) Yes, you sometimes have difficulty concentrating, like your brain is in a fog. (Leave out the ectoplasm, he'd never believe in the paranormal.) From time to time you feel what you could only describe as something restless, but you rarely feel slowed. (Don't say it's only when your daughter is crying and you're not sure if you left the bars of her crib down; you feel an invisible hand holding your leg when you try to walk down the hallway. You can't explain how, last night after you drove home, you thought you saw the weeping woman in the bathroom, with eyes that were mostly just dark sockets, and tangled black hair that hasn't seen a shower in days, maybe weeks.) No, you never feel low in spirits. Not with your daughter around. How could you?

It's possible that you could have the blues. (But you are careful; you don't mention blue orbs, the ones that show up in whatever picture you try taking of your daughter to send to your husband in New York or LA or Toronto. You don't mention when you try to sleep at night there is always blue light, whether from orbs or computer screens with pictures of dead-baby albatross chicks, stomachs full of bright plastic their mothers mistook for shrimp, pictures of hives missing adult bees with larva still unhatched, pictures of fewer and fewer swallows migrating across a sky too early for their eggs to be laid and their young to find food. What's happening can't be natural; in the blue light you read how the young won't survive.) Your doctor says it happens to a lot of women. Your doctor says that naturally, you'll start feeling better soon. Of course you'll be fine. (You have to be fine. If you tell him about the watermelon, he might think you're not a natural. He might think there's something missing. He might think, if you have something missing, you shouldn't have your baby anymore.)

* * *

It's nothing, and you're fine. Everything is fine; nothing bad really happened. Your husband says you're fine, sitting across from you in the living room, offering you a paper bag. There's no reason to panic (even when the weeping woman is still inside your house), just try to breathe (even when she holds you down on your bed, her weight on top of your chest when you hear your daughter crying in the middle of the afternoon). In through your nose, out through your mouth. (Even when you try to breathe, you get a mouthful of her long dark hair followed by the rain. It's easy to mistake the sound of a thumping heart for a record player, the groove of a record for what's always happened, the end of a record for white noise, white noise for what isn't there.) You'll be fine. You're a good mom. (Even if yesterday afternoon the weeping woman left the stove on, made a tiny fire break out, and what kind of mother hesitates to smother it, even if only for a second, what kind of mother doesn't immediately run to grab her daughter, thinking instead, with relief, of the Bell Witch haunting, how in pictures of children in front of her cave, the children always disappear?) You'll try to be fine, even if your husband has to go away again. If you have any problems, you should try reaching out to your mother-in-law. Try to see how lucky you are. *You should try leaving your newborn daughter at home all the time.* Try seeing how hard this is for him too. (You're trying, but even your neighbor saw the weeping woman the other day as you went outside to take out the burned remains of one bottle with the odour of sour milk still on your clothes. You're trying to be fine; you said you're fine and she said, *Don't give me that. I have twin boys. I know what ichor looks like.*) You know he has to go; you know this is what you should expect. Of course you'll be fine. You're a good mom. Before he leaves, your husband gives you two violets growing in a bell jar. He says, *I thought we could try again.* Of course you want to. Your husband looks at your daughter, sleeping in his arms in a onesie you could only find in lemon. He says, *I know you wouldn't want this to change.* Of course all this is what you wanted.

The afternoon he leaves again, in a small moment alone in the bathtub, the weeping woman's hair covers your face, ties your hands behind your back. It wraps itself around your neck, the same way a seagull will always lose to six-pack rings. It's nothing, then it isn't, but you can almost sleep as it pulls you under.

*   *   *

It isn't nothing; it's not supposed to happen. It isn't just the wind, or a bicycle turned upside down, tire spinning underneath a piece of stretched-out silk. It's not just dolphin or sea-lion cries run through a vocoder, or a cutting of black plastic garbage bags into thin strips, then burning them into an unearthly whine as they drip to the ground. It isn't just that things are upside down, a warming Arctic means colder winters down south, instead of a playpen and toys everywhere, the living room becomes an Escher painting. The lamps levitate, the sofa drifts towards the ceiling, the violets in their bell jar hang like purple bats, or stalactites carved from the last ice age. It's not supposed to happen, but the weeping woman throws things: your daughter's toys that you step over, a watering can, the shears you are supposed to use to deadhead the violets in the bell jar but can't seem to see yourself doing. It's not supposed to happen; this isn't what you want for your daughter and you need to get out of this place. It's not what you expected; you even call your mother-in-law to say you need a change, you need to stay there with your daughter tonight. It's not supposed to happen but just as you're about to leave the weeping woman misplaces the bags you packed, your daughter's diapers, a change of clothes, everything except the dying violets in their bell jar. You're trying to get out of this place but you just changed your daughter and she needs changing again and you needed to leave ten minutes ago and somehow time has rewound itself so that every time you get to the door you go back to where you started from. You don't know what it is that lets you finally leave the house; in the case of the Amityville ghost boy it was a cameraman named Paul wearing the same striped shirt, but that doesn't explain a mother levitating from her bed so far off the ground her children couldn't find her hand. It isn't nothing; in the case of the Enfield poltergeist, Jane's mother was trapped by a heavy oak dresser in the bedroom and you can't see the Christmas lights that are all lit up on the front porch of the old Victorian in the headlights of your car. It's not fine; it's the weeping woman that gets in the front seat of your car this time, roughly buckles your daughter in beside her where she isn't supposed to be. You can't see the lights and no one saw how Jane's mother was trapped, but your neighbor sees your daughter in the front seat of your car. You could have used some metal wind chimes, laid them on a surface then moved a bottle over them. You could have filled some small glass vials with water and placed them with some coins inside a pillowcase. But that's not what really happens. You're really the weeping woman and when your daughter cries again, the weeping woman throws the bell jar with its violets against the windshield, just above your daughter's head. That's what makes the sound of breaking glass. That's what makes your terrier keep barking. That's what makes your daughter scream in fear. That's what makes your neighbor knock on the car window, and the weeping woman opens it. She says you're fine. Your daughter's fine. The windshield is not fine; the violets are not fine and neither is the bell jar. Neither are the turtles and the fruit and the flowers with their disappearing bees. But your daughter is not a violet, the weeping woman tells your neighbor. Your daughter is not a watermelon. Your daughter is a lemon and your neighbor sees the weeping woman is real. She says she should go; your neighbor will take your daughter, and you ask her why but you know she sees what could happen because it shouldn't. *You do what you can,* she says. It shouldn't happen. But if Jane's mother was trapped, and with a haunting like that, what could she do when a force she couldn't quite understand lifted up and shook her daughter, then threw her violently across the room?

Your neighbor will take you to the hospital. Your neighbor holds out her arms; you're not fine. *It's going to be okay. You can give her to me.* The weeping woman holds on to your daughter, bends down to kiss her. *Just let her go,* you neighbor says, opening the car door, *you need to let her go.* To make a believable kissing sound, you could wet your lips with a glass of water, put your mouth slowly on the underside of your forearm, the part with very little hair. But to make a believable kissing sound as the weeping woman you can't. It's nothing. You give your daughter to your neighbor; she holds your daughter in her arms and you get out of the car. *You're fine dear, it's fine now.* You get out of your car crying and she says, *Don't feel bad. You're doing what you can. You can only do what you can.* You get out of your car, and not the weeping woman. From the back seat of your neighbor's van you can see the Christmas lights on the porch, twinkling, even if they're distant. You feel the thumping of the bass from a song she puts on the radio; you feel your heartbeat start to slow to match it, and it is real, no mistaking it.

* * *

The next time you see the weeping woman she is an emergency-room chair, then a long day while you watch the blue of TV screens in the hospital, then your husband asking if you feel better now, or a forgotten prescription that you only refill later, or the baby swallow you have to explain to your daughter that she shouldn't have touched because her mother won't take it back to the nest anymore. The weeping woman is the clump of black hair you clean out of the bathtub drain some mornings. Leave out the part where you pretend you don't see it moving. Leave out the part where you pretend. You take the hair and tie it with a blue ribbon and when it dances on the windowsill of your bedroom and your daughter comes to find you because she wants a glass of lemonade; she sees it too. She asks you what it is. You don't tell her about jellyfish ghosts and dead turtles. You don't tell her it's unlikely the watermelon seeds she planted in the windowsill garden will grow to be a watermelon; she told you when you planted them that she learned in school that she would need to take care of the earth to make the seeds grow. So you tell her the hair is like the baby swallow and you watch it dance together, to the sound of the bass on the radio. You say you'll get her lemonade; you want to say that lemons will survive. You want to say sometimes you are just learning to let things go. You both watch the hair dance until a draft catches it, and the thin strands separate, carried out the window into the ocean maybe, dissolving into almost nothing, carried by what could almost be the wind.

PAOLA FERRANTE'S *debut poetry collection,* What to Wear When Surviving A Lion Attack, *was shortlisted for the 2020 Gerald Lampert Memorial Award. She was longlisted for the 2020 Journey Prize and won* The New Quarterly's

2019 Peter Hinchcliffe Fiction Award, Grain's *2020 prize for Poetry and* Room's *2018 prize for Fiction. She was also an Honorable Mention for* The North American Review's *2020 Kurt Vonnegut prize. Her work has appeared, or is forthcoming, in* PRISM International, CV2, The Journey Prize Stories *32, and elsewhere. She is the Poetry Editor at* Minola Review *and resides in Toronto, Canada.*

Cicada Summer

Emma Eun-joo Choi

It was the hottest summer in a decade, the summer after my freshman year of college, the summer you were in a psych ward in California and I sat stewing at home in Virginia. It was cicada summer, come to us again after seventeen years, and the ground glittered with the shells of the bugs, every surface teeming with cicadas, eating, molting, and eating again.

They were all anyone could talk about. Every segment on the local news featured footage of the bugs, every grocery store line hummed with news: they were clogging up the drain, eating up the lawn, disturbing the night with their incessant screeching. Their sound swallowed up the night sky. Every time the sun went down they rose up their voices to a bone-squeaking screech, ringing through the solid summer air, making the walls of each house hum with the vibrations. It was as if the cicadas had overridden the rhythm of our town, eating away until they could calibrate it to their own. We were marching to the beat of an alien drum, dancing to a song sung backward.

They were not here and then they were. Bursting out of silence and into endless noise. They came from the deepest roots of trees, from the ground, from a buried place.

*   *   *

I spent my days drifting around the house. Sometimes I'd lie on the floor for hours at a time, just lie there and feel the heat swirl over my skin, feel the sunlight on my eyelids as the sun moved through the windows, listen to the sound of weak voices filter up through the floor. I heard my name but it wasn't me. I felt my muscles clench and unclench again and again, the ever-present flutter in my chest, the grinding of my teeth, but it wasn't me.

My mother tried to get me off the floor by giving me tasks. She'd walk into my room with a basket of laundry. She'd ask me for groceries, for postage stamps, if I could send a package to Aunt Kate. She'd stand in the doorway with her hand on the frame and ask, Don't you want to do anything? Don't you get tired of just lying around? I looked at her upside down from my place on the rug. No, I said.

I went on like this for weeks, sweating slowly, staring at my phone, lying on my bedroom floor, counting each hour as it dripped off my fingers. And then one day I stood up and walked out the back door, for no reason but to walk, and I walked out of the house and into the forest.

*   *   *

It was just a house. A house with white clapboards and a wide porch that wrapped around the entire perimeter of the structure. The porch was filled with chairs of all sizes, rocking chairs and children's chairs, highchairs and armchairs, chairs meant for both sitting and just seeing. It was a house with a long driveway but no tire marks in the gravel. As I walked up the driveway I tried to look for lights in the windows but the curtains were drawn tight and when I knocked, nobody answered.

There must have been nearly a hundred chairs up on that porch. I walked through the narrow spaces between them and sometimes I sat down. They held me and didn't break. There was no breeze to sway the rocking chairs, only the wet heat that hung on my shoulders like a damp coat, that sat in the chairs and made it all silent.

All silent except for the wails of the cicadas. Again and again, crying out together into the solid heat of the morning, wave after wave of sound making the floorboards hum with vibration, my teeth ache with the shrieks. And in the yard of this house the cicadas were everywhere. Everywhere: a carpet of sound and movement, a blinding floor of shells sparkling in the sunlight. They surrounded the house on any part that was grass and wailed again and again. And when I sat down by the front steps they started to move. Churning in circles in slow motion, lugging their small bodies through sugar syrup starting to cool. They followed each other, tracing the same lines, marching to a place they'd been to before. I sat on the steps and watched them spin in slow circles until the sun rose too high and the air thickened to a solid and I couldn't take it—the heat forced me back to the forest.

* * *

Each day I came and each day they changed course. Only slightly, but just enough that I could notice. The pattern was almost imperceptible. Occasionally bugs would stray out of line, moving towards the middle or the outskirts, giving the illusion of randomness again. But every day they made something new. A spiral. A square. A shape without a name. I came every morning and sat on those steps and nobody ever came up the driveway, never opened the door or called out the window. I never did anything or tried to interfere. I only sat there until I couldn't bear the heat any longer. I only sat and waited for the cicadas to change course.

* * *

One day I came home to find my mother waiting for me in the kitchen.

Where have you been going? she asked, and I just shrugged.

Just walking, I said.

She shook her head, set her coffee on the table.

I found you a job at the local newspaper, she said. You start on Monday.

What?

You can't just lie around at home all day, she said. You're nineteen years old. You should be making money for when you go back to school.

You don't get to tell me what I have to do, I said. I'm a—

She cut me off with a sigh.

Please, she said, please just try it. You might even like it. I just—it just hurts me to see you like this, it really does. Just go for one day and if you hate it you can quit—you're right, you're an adult now. All I ask is that you give it a chance, okay? Please?

When I didn't reply she looked at me sadly, reluctantly picking up her mug to walk out of the kitchen. My feet clung to the ground with a layer of sweat. A trickle ran down my forehead into the corner of my mouth.

* * *

The newsroom was in a large, poorly air-conditioned room on Church Street. On my first day a very enthusiastic man greeted me and introduced himself as my mom's friend. He showed me my desk, the restroom, the small coffee maker. He introduced me to the other writers, each middle aged and easily forgettable. He started talking to me about the work they did there, about deadlines and interviewing policy and human-interest stories. Outside, the clicking of the cicadas pushed against the window. It was nearing a hundred degrees. It was a wet, pressing heat that sat heavy in the weak sky. I looked out the window and tried to figure out which way was west. I thought about wildfires. About air hot enough to melt shells.

—the library is always a good place to start, although for this particular case it could be more useful to . . .

I blinked. Sorry, I said. Could you repeat that last part?

The man—Elliot—stopped talking and smiled. If he could tell I hadn't been listening he didn't show it.

Here, it's all in the file. He handed me a green folder with the words *Human Interest—Historical* marked on it in thick permanent marker. Basically, we'd love you to do some research and find the guy in the picture and write a piece about it. We found a bunch of these kinds of photos deep in our archives and we thought it would be fun to do a series on town history! He smiled. He had a kind smile. I felt bad about not listening.

Anyways, good luck! Welcome to the team!

I sat down at my desk and opened the folder. Slipped inside the front pocket was a worn black-and-white photo about the size of my palm.

A man sat at a bar. He wore a suit, his hair neat and slicked back, one foot on the rung of the stool and the other on the floor. He held a drink and smiled at someone off camera, his whole face lit up with a grin. It was a simple photo. There was a bar and a stool and drink and a man and the thing he was looking at. A white border all around. I stared at the margin, willing the figure to come into view. His mouth hung slightly open. He looked as if he was about to say a name.

* * *

The cicadas were moving a little faster than before, scuttling over each other to make little piles that shivered and then fell down. I sat on the steps of the house until the sun started to set over the willow trees. I thought about the photo. The cicadas kept making piles. Building up and falling down. Up and down and up again.

* * *

The next day I drove to the only bar in town to ask the owner about the photo. It was 11 a.m. and the bar was empty—there was only a lone bartender and the flat stench of cigarettes in every corner. I approached the bar, pulling the straps of my tote bag higher onto my shoulder.

Hi, I said. Is the owner in?

The man looked up. He looked only a little bit older than me—maybe five years or so. His pencil was frozen in the middle of a half-filled Sudoku grid. He wore a Virginia Tech t-shirt with a hole in the shoulder.

Sorry, he said, he's out. I can help you, though.

I pulled the photo from my bag and explained to him my assignment. He took the photo and held it up to the dim light. He looked at it for a few moments, his eyes dancing rapidly. I tried to place him from somewhere in my memory, to recognize him from high school, the grocery store, church. But I couldn't find him anywhere. He was just some guy.

He handed it back to me, shaking his head.

Sorry, he said. I don't think that was taken here. See? He tapped the back mirrors in the photo. We didn't get those kinds of mirrors until a few years ago.

I put the folder back in my bag and started to thank him for his time anyways, but he kept looking at me with his furrowed forehead.

Why? Is he famous or something? he asked, cutting me off.

I blinked.

No, I said. He's just someone I'm supposed to find.

Okay, he said. You just made it sound like he was someone important.

He looked back down at his Sudoku.

Well . . . He looked back up. I cleared my throat. Well, you never know, right? Maybe he is someone important or at least . . . I took out the picture again. Look, I said, doesn't it look like he's talking to someone important?

He took the photo again and brought it closer to his face. Yeah, he said after a moment. Yeah, I can see that.

He put down the photo and seemed to think for a moment. He reached down under the counter and pulled out a thick binder, flipping through the tabs. With a snap, he undid the rings and took out a page of paper.

Here, he said. Rob—my boss—keeps a running list of the competition around us. I think sometimes he orders taxis to take drunks to the other bars. I'm sure he won't mind you taking a copy.

I took it and looked over the contents. There were about ten names and addresses on the page.

Thank you, I said. I really appreciate it.

No problem, he said. I hope you find him.

*   *   *

My mother met me at the door when I got back home.

Welcome home, honey! She sniffed—frowned. You smell like cigarettes.

I tossed my bag onto the kitchen table and started to head upstairs.

Wait, she said, and I turned around. She looked at me with wide, hopeful eyes. For a moment I felt bad.

How was your first day? she asked. Did they give you anything interesting?

It was fine, I said. They put me on a research assignment.

She smiled so wide it hurt my face.

That's awesome! Wow!

I smiled and started to turn around. She started to take a step forward and stopped herself.

Wait, she said. Are you doing okay?

Yeah, I said.

She kept looking at me. I turned around and walked up the stairs.

*   *   *

The cicadas learned how to build upon themselves, making strange sculptures that glittered in the sun. I began to dream of cicadas. I watched them spell out long cursive sentences in floating grass, held them in my hands as they danced between my fingers. At night the cicadas sang together in great big waves of screeches. Their cries filtered into my dreams, the ringing of their cries manifested as a phone made out of their wings that always rang but I could never reach, never even touch.

*   *   *

Each day I drove to another bar. At every bar I found another man and I showed him the photo and he shook his head. He gave me the names and addresses of more bars, some of which were already on my list, some of which were not. Every day I drove down long highways in heat-pressed Virginia searching for a shack along the road, a little town with a name only a little different than mine. All the towns began looking the same: a few streets with shops and buildings and, surrounding, sprawling roads leading to houses and farms, roads leading to more roads. Finally, I found a bar with a man who said yes. It was the eleventh, or the sixteenth, or the thirtieth bar I went to but when he said yes it became the first. Everything was new again—even the dirty countertop seemed clean and beautiful. His father was the owner back in the sixties. It was his back that was in the edge of the photo. He wrote down the address of a retirement home and the name John Brody.

There's not a lot of him left, he warned me. I wouldn't expect too much from him.

Thank you, I said. This is amazing.

* * *

They were making something. They formed the same structure each time I came, climbing higher and higher until something buckled and they all collapsed. They were getting louder. They were so loud my ears could barely take it. Screaming together in one voice, one exhausting cry. My bones ached and I sat there and watched them. I waited for someone to come home.

* * *

The retirement home smelled like cotton and cold air. The nurse led me to the farthest bedroom down the hallway and inside were four walls painted sage green, a painting of vague flowers, and a man with skin like rice paper.

Mr. Brody? I asked. He was looking out the window where cicadas were covering a tree.

There are so many, he said. So many.

Yes, I said. It's incredible.

He looked at me. You weren't here for the last one, I see.

I took a seat by his bedside.

No.

Hmm, he said, and looked back out the window. Well there were a lot more last time, I can tell you that. He looked back at me. Say, do you know where they come from?

No, I said. I waited for him to tell me but he just looked back outside. Slowly, I took out the photo and placed it in his lap.

Mr. Brody, I said, trying to catch his eye. I was wondering if you knew who this man is? Your son, Andy, told me to ask you.

He looked at the photo. He picked it up and held it near his face. His hand was translucent in the fluorescent ceiling light. The veins webbed down his knuckle—purple and white.

Say, he said. How's Adelaide doing? Been a while since I've seen her in here. She and James still living on Maple?

James, I thought.

I don't know, I said.

He smiled.

What a wonderful girl, he said. She was always humming that song . . . how did it go again?

He started humming something slow. His voice was sandy, like it needed a good shake. He hummed a few bars and stopped. He looked out the window again.

Look at that, he said. They're really everywhere.

He looked at me.

Do you know where they come from?

* * *

I saw a face in the curve of a mound. I stood up and leaned against the railing, straining against the wall of heat to look, but the mounds kept shifting and the impression was gone. I sat back down.

* * *

There were a hundred Jameses in the phone book but only one Adelaide. She lived on Maple Street in the town next to mine. It wasn't hard to copy down her address onto my phone or to find the address on the navigation. It wasn't hard to drive the ten minutes to her house or to drive down the long driveway toward the single-story yellow house. And yet I sat in the driveway for half an hour just staring at the garage, my heart thudding a strange rhythm in my chest. I waited for something to happen, for the door to open or the lights to turn off. But nothing happened. It was up to me. I looked at the picture and I waited for him to look at me. To look at me and see me.

Finally, I unbuckled my seat belt and took a deep breath. For some reason I felt like crying. I took more deep breaths and stepped out of the car—the crunching of cicadas beneath my feet settling deep into my ears. I walked up to the door and knocked once. I breathed. I waited.

The woman who opened the door was short—maybe five feet—and wore a yellow housecoat that swept down to her ankles. She had a sweet, pleasant face and smiled up at me with waxy pink lips.

Hi! she said, her voice high and fragile. Can I help you?

I blinked. I remembered to smile.

Hi! I'm from the *Appleton Herald*. I actually, um . . . I thrust the photo toward her. Is this your husband?

Adelaide took the photo and her hand went to her mouth. Her eyes shone as she looked back up at me with a huge smile across her face.

It is! She looked at it again. Oh my. He's so young here.

I waited for her to turn back to the house and call out his name, to tell me to wait there one second or even to come in, but she just stood there with her hand on her heart and looked at the picture.

This must've been . . . well it must've been 1968. Jim only had that suit for a year, you know. He spilled red wine all over it! She threw her head back and laughed a loud, ringing laugh. Oh wow. Where did you get this?

I don't know, I said. My editor just told me to find him.

Adelaide's face fell.

I'm so sorry, Adelaide said. Oh, I'm so sorry. Jim passed away a few years ago.

I took a step back.

I'm sorry, dear. Oh, I'm so sorry.

*   *   *

The cicadas were silent. They didn't make a sound and they didn't move. They sat on the ground as I stood on the steps of the house and waited for them to speak. The silence was the worst thing I'd ever heard. It was the sound of the space between sentences, of the white page underneath. I felt it crammed into my ears, crawling over my skin, and I couldn't stand it. I couldn't stand the stillness, the way the trees sat frozen as if they had never heard of wind, the way the heat held everything in its single solid space, and I couldn't stand it. I couldn't move. I stood there in that terrible silence, the excruciating stillness of it all, between the cicadas sitting motionless in the yard and the house just as silent, among all the chairs that stayed empty, and finally, just as I opened my mouth to scream, the phone rang.

I shut my mouth

The phone kept ringing.

I looked back at the house and the windows were still empty. There were no tire marks in the gravel and the door was still shut. The phone kept on ringing. I stood up and walked to the door, knocking a few times and waiting for the sound of footsteps. I tried the handle and it turned. I opened the door and stepped inside.

It was a home without people. There was a kitchen with a clean counter and floors with few stains. There was a couch and an armchair and a basket with blankets. There was a bookshelf with some books, a rug, a ceiling fan and tall lamps. I stood in the doorway, my breath coming in uneven pulls, as I surveyed the house, this collection of rooms and empty space.

The phone was still ringing. I crossed the floor to where the landline hung on the wall. I picked it up and it was you.

Hi baby. Your voice faltered, shook. It's me.

I staggered back to lean on the wall.

I heard you take a breath, heard it rattle in your throat as you let it go.

I'm coming home tomorrow, you said.

I began to cry.

Oh baby, you said. Baby. I'm sorry I didn't call. I'm sorry. I know I said I would. I just didn't know . . . I couldn't . . .

Outside, the sound of cicadas began to rise. At first as a pale whisper, then growing louder. Bigger. A million voices calling out from the grass, the trees, the bushes, the sky. The sky was orange with dusk and the clouds shook with the cicadas' sound, trembling like tissue paper against the smothering heat. The cicadas were screaming and the walls were alight with vibrations and I, standing inside them, shaking too, rocking like a rocking chair on the hard wooden floor as I crushed the phone into my ear and my hand into my chest and wept into the floorboards.

I love you, I said.

I love you. You said it like you were letting out a long breath. I love you so much.

I slid down the wall to the floor, my legs splayed out before me. And I cried there, my back convulsing inside that shaking house, and you cried, too, your breathing cracking through the phone and we cried together. And when the cicadas came through the door I didn't even look up. They came in as they shaped themselves into a pillar, a mass, a man. Standing before me. A man glittering and seething with sound. And he came to me and knelt on the ground, here at last in his final shape, ready to be seen and found.

EMMA EUN-JOO CHOI is a playwright and fiction writer from Vienna, Virginia. Her fiction has been featured in publications including Passages North, Jelly Bucket Magazine, *and* The Harvard Advocate, *and her plays have been professionally produced in DC and New York City. Emma is a current student at Harvard College studying English, where she also performs comedy.*

Whitney in the Real World

Stephanie Pushaw

Whitney went to Marin's office with that scoured-out feeling in her stomach, like the thin-cut skin of a jack-o'-lantern: shaved close to let the light through, rot accumulating slowly on the inside walls. She'd put on weight, letting the scale tip wine-ward more than not, despite advice from her tired doctor who'd showed her a cirrhotic liver that looked like foie gras. The ramifications hammered her down, sweat struggling through her caked contouring, the cheekbones mere suggestions now. The miserably expensive chair. The settling weight of her body burdening the synthetic white leather. Blue light from the river cast its mute judgment through the glass; buildings outside swayed at their tops, silver gray and slim, bright figures dotting the rooftop bars and gardens. Sunlight stopped where the tinted glass began. Inside was Marin's special calculated glow, pure and even as a cleanser, from an invisible source embedded along the corners where the walls met the ceiling. Marin was looking at her through those big glasses, the ones she claimed were vintage. They weren't. It was common knowledge, unsubstantiated but unsurprising: a little chip wired to the inside of the right temple, a chip that sent messages to the lenses. Messages like: 36-24-36, I want lots of pretty chicks. (That old song. That ancient mantra.) Messages like: skin problems, beer belly, badly waxed legs. Messages that affected raises, and bonuses, and gigs. Messages you didn't really want to be plastered over your real-time self as Marin appraised you through her two layers: green contacts concealing the muddy eyes her skin tone suggested she'd been born with, and then the other layer, the one that saw you for everything you were.

"Whitney," Marin said, showing a new tooth gem, maybe emerald.

"Hi," Whitney said, aware as she'd settled that her skirt, unflatteringly tight, had ridden up and revealed the corners of her unshaved kneecaps. The skirt was supposed to cover them. She crossed her legs, new sheens of sweat peeling away from the white leather as she moved. Marin asked her if she was happy these days. Whitney was, and she said so. This was a good job. She went home to a bed gleefully empty and dressed in gray linen, and an apartment which she paid for with nobody's help.

"Because if you wanted a different one," Marin said, "like one without so much screen time, one more behind the scenes, maybe we could do that."

The reality department. Slipping clumsily into the ranks of the girls who used the discreet suites on the sixtieth floor, those monolithic black glass walls at which sound and sight stopped. Noise cancelling. Glass doors flush with glass walls, melting open at the touch of a button down the hall in security. Those suites were exclusively for after-hours use; the cameras in there went only to security, and the footage automatically erased after each session. Security couldn't bring phones into the booth, either, so nobody could tape the live feed. Whenever a client used those suites, elevator operations to that floor were temporarily suspended.

"Marin," Whitney said, with a measured confidence she did not feel, "I love my job. I know I'm maybe not in the best shape right now for the shoot next month." She swallowed her unsaid *but*. They both knew there wasn't one.

Marin looked at her long enough to coax the silence louder. Pushed her glasses up, finally, and it was like watching someone unscrew a prosthetic. Her eyes were those of a frog Whitney had seen on the internet, green and staring, the entire process so unbearably intimate Whitney had to look away. Marin's hands were blinged out in slim golden rings, so many it was impossible to know if any one of them signified anything: marriage, possession, promises. No fingers were naked. Her nails were glowing. Microstudding. Some of the reality girls got it done. They put gems or liquid gold or something under the top layer of clear polish.

"If you can get yourself there," Marin said, "I think we'd both be really happy."

That was it? She shifted in her seat, sticking morbidly to its leather, and opened her mouth to say something starting with, "so," but "I think, between you and me," preinterrupted Marin, visibly bored, sliding one glimmering fingertip down the surface of her desk, "it's best to avoid the fitness center if you can get it under control on your own. It can be very demoralizing." Here she looked up, her finger paused, and flipped her head in a quick jerk so her glasses slid back onto her face. "It would be great if you could take this one on yourself."

Relief dizzy, Whitney stood up, meal-planning in her head: she would do the horrible liquid stuff, she would take the supplement pills, she would avoid and avoid and avoid all the things she turned to for a slight jolt of pointless happiness. Marin gave her Dr. Matsumara's number. She visited him the next day. They spoke for six minutes and she left with a prescription for something she was supposed to take with a full glass of water and supplement with guided meditation and auto-acupuncture. "You can drink," Matsumara said, though she hadn't asked. "But make it one or two, once a week. Glasses, not bottles," he said, laughing, and she laughed with him, as though they both shared this secret joke, sitting high on a moral mountaintop where nobody would ever consider housing a bottle of chardonnay to herself one night in front of old game shows.

In the elevator up to her car she could feel it, a new and distasteful urge she'd been attempting to eradicate, coming back strong: her mind angling, already, toward that one drink she was allowed per week. A martini, maybe, swimming in the reek of olive, at the white bar of the microtel under her apartment. Or a glass of something stout and comfortable, sipped at the wooden picnic table on the back patio at Thelma's. It was pointless to deny it now: she'd traded control of her brain, ceded it over to the sweet reek of ethanol. The week itself, dragging all its inevitable indignities, would be a long and dismal lead-up to this thirty-minute session of release.

But to her surprise, the pills worked beautifully. She no longer woke up and immediately panged with longing to return to sleep. The one or two drinks a week turned out to be kind of fun, even: she savored them, now. They were luxuries—chardonnay sliding around her brain, layering itself right below her skin, soft and golden and protective; a vodka soda with a bright wedge of lime brightening her neurons momentarily. She went to the microtel on Fridays, sometimes meeting people, sometimes drinking alone but surrounded, and it had become something like a ceremony for her: something that kept her tethered, that made the loud banging in her skull stutter to a halt.

Makeup or no makeup; wide trousers or the kind of tight dress that spanned decades in its appeal. It never mattered. She *glew*—it wasn't the right word for the past tense of glow, but it was how she felt. She felt as though she glew. Then she went back home and sought sleep the natural way. Tossing, turning, brain wired tight as a motherboard. But in control. Come morning she'd slug a fat pill down with a full glass of water, then sit, for thirty minutes, eyes closed, headphones in, before a screen that in singsong reminded her to breathe.

*   *   *

Lightbulbs hanging naked above the bar, blazing their standard brightness over skin and stemless glassware. More women than men, and Charlie didn't like it. It made him feel off-kilter—that they were all real people, and here he was, also real but never feeling less so. Like a servant entering a harem with downcast eyes, bearing, on a silver tray, liqueurs and lubes.

What a shitty metaphor. In a harem, the girls had to be there. They were acting, acting, all the time, acting like they liked the old sultan or whoever grabbing their ass as they walked too close to his throne, acting like he was capable of bringing them all to orgasm with the merest caress, the most inadvisably premature dry thrust. He supposed even if the sultan were young and hot they'd still be acting, because who would bother to fall in love with someone who you knew had bought you, along with other girls? Who would bother to fall in love with someone who *had* so many girls?

He was, for the first time in a long time, conscious of what he was wearing. Because although there were more women than men, there were still men, and they all looked at ease in their uniforms, the geometry of shirt and jacket squaring away the chest, the sharp crease of khaki or radiating cool of denim. Charlie used to know what to wear to go out, used to know what was acceptable for people. It was the first time in months he'd had to put together an outfit, rather than absentmindedly pulling on whatever was around if he needed to walk to one of those dinosaur restaurants that didn't deliver. Those archaic hipster joints. McCallen's, which was, despite the name, Vietnamese. No delivery, no takeout, eat-in only under these horrific lights that made everyone look like reanimated corpses. Radiant, corpse-reviving lemongrass soup.

And when he went there it didn't matter what he wore, flannel or yellowing white tank top or marinara-stained cords or what, because everyone there was like him: alone with their peanut sauce, their daikon, their banh mi with carrot shreds flaking out the corners. Alone and avoiding eye contact under that hospital strip lighting. It was soothing, warming, anonymous. He loved it. But now. His pony-hair jacket, which had seemed so invaluable in the past; his corduroys, tight and crease worn, which now felt like he'd dug them out of a crypt or something.

They didn't smell, but he imagined they looked like they smelled. It had, he guessed, been a minute since he'd done the thing: pushed back the curtains, entered the great blinding expanse that was Other People. None of the men looked like him. None of them were wearing anything he had in his closet. He felt suddenly, keenly aware of the snake tattoo wrapping his wrist; felt its outline as sharply as though it were still red rimmed and wrapped in plastic. And oh, these girls: they seemed as close to CGI as it were possible for humans to get; their faces all smooth planes dotted with sculpture gardens, everything locked down, refined, exacerbated. They all had heartbreaking eyebrows.

Easy laughter sparked behind him and he started. Low, slinking, paranoid: he did not know why he was here, began to cast the old weary hatred back onto himself. Maybe it was like the Playboy Mansion. Right. Like being some weird landscaper at the Playboy Mansion, fielding derisive looks and hand-cupped laughter from girls on their way to the pool. He'd read some things—exposes and memoirs, excerpted online. He'd read them to see if they had pictures, but, when they hadn't, somehow read on, in a fugue of displaced hatred. All the stories seemed fake. Likely tossed out by some disgruntled bunnies who hadn't dug the way the old guy had to take pills to get his equipment working. Girls who couldn't accept that someone, even an octogenarian, wouldn't get it up for them—so they wrote revenge pieces alleging abuse, gaslighting, a whole host of stuff you'd have just figured, no matter how dumb, they'd have to be at least be smart enough to anticipate.

He wondered if the women here could sense how much he hated them: their long brown legs, their stark collarbones you could hang things from. How much he hated their lipstick, their hair, their dangling jewels and the visible smalls of their backs, their jutting butts and treadmilled calves, their feet strapped into complicated shoes. One of them looked at him. He smiled inadvertently. She didn't look appalled, but shifted her smile to some overshoulder ghost.

There was, he thought, maybe something to be said for harems, or houses with hired hot girls: those situations were transactional.

There were terms. He understood, at least in the abstract, how those might work. It was basically acting. Acting, if not exactly loving, at least undisgusted. And putting out. This was different. This was real life, boy, he thought, now, inexplicably face to face with it. Real life, and he moved through it timid and miserable, the way all of his type of person seemed to (the ones who stayed inside, the ones who relied on scheduled deliveries, on applications understanding them with tenderness), and if he occasionally brushed up against the other type of person, the ones who weaponized their bodies and peacocked in cowl-draped backless satin—well, he was only human. For better or for worse. He longed for beauty to touch him; longed for its languid needle to slip into his skin, to pulse something generous and warm into that mysterious bundle of blood-wires that hummed constantly inside like a low-grade sub-cutaneous fever. There were times he'd felt close to beauty. Times when the downward sweep of lashes in candlelight cast rushing shadows over his forearm and he felt a hitch in his heart. Times when lips opened near enough his ear to prickle all his neck hairs awake. Times when he looked down at crushed-closed eyelids and counted the creases where the eyeshadow collected, its brown or gold shimmer escaping, for a moment, the confines of perfection; sometimes, afterward, he imagined finding it on his pillow. Of course, he never did. These memories, precious as the ring he'd stolen from Lauren Leo back in tenth grade, the thick one with the opal and the little embossed double Ls. He came across it shoved in the back of a bathroom drawer the other day, and thought of her again, the stuck image in his mind: their house had backed onto the Leos, and his bedroom overlooked the pool. Her areolas, strikingly brown against the fabric of her white triangle top, and the smooth peaks of her hipbones. These memories, which he played back at will, but not too frequently—once every six months, maybe, lest they lose their vitality. These memories, which were as real as real memories. Or maybe even more real, since by now everybody knew memories could be bought.

Unsure of what people ordered, he ordered what he usually had sent to him at home: a beer from Wisconsin named after an ancient saint. The payment stymied him momentarily, but he remembered, like a whisper from a long time ago, the process: you tapped the back of your watch on the reader, and if you had enough money in your account, it hummed from red to green. He had enough money. He always did. Money was never the problem.

The beer seemed sweeter poured into a glass, its effect maybe a little stronger, here under the strange, loud halos. He drank from it, held it up to the warm light, studied it, conscious as a cinematographer of how deliberate he must look. Not that anyone was looking. It was dark gold; a thin foam sat at its top; the sips he'd taken, three or four, pooled themselves with incredible swiftness in his stomach, vibing upward to his brain, and he felt almost drunk. But that was impossible. The beer had the same alcohol per volume as it did at home, when he slit the weekly delivery box open with one of the knives he'd never used for any other purpose, when he cracked the bottles with the back of a vintage corkscrew. It entered his bloodstream the same; it was processed by his liver the same, with a minimum of outcry, since he knew about water, and pacing, and sleep.

If anything, he figured (now leaning with an uneasy elbow against the slick bar, hoping that the bar was just slick with some faddish new polymer and his pony-hair jacket wasn't collecting beer-grease and whiskey-spit) he was feeling so unsteady already—what with being in this place, this strange and miserably bright place—that the beer was just hitting him harder in his mind. A lot of things were psychological like that. It was one of the reasons he tried not to leave the house. In the house, he knew how everything worked. He finished the beer without tasting it. He felt better: loose, maybe ready to try a conversation. He looked around, toying with a smile that threatened to rise to his lips, swallowing down some strange new optimism that leapt unbidden to his throat. And, like some unseen directing deity had just kicked her from the wings, he saw her—star of his playback fantasies, woman he loved, had loved since she was introduced, had cloven to above all her peers. At first she was hard to make out, just one of the burnished, slippery clientele: tossed hair, white teethed, every eyebrow hair brushed individually and coated in something that made light stop at their borders like black holes. Then: a quick half-turn in something back-cupping and black, her icy hair catching the light that spilled from one of the buckets; a flash of eyes that bored into him like a sonic boom, like the metal mesh that warped the gun to the guy's hand in *Videodrome*. And he saw her, in that second, and recognized her face, and it wasn't like a movie. It was nothing like a movie. He was gut-punched, sideswiped, bruised along the map of his vitals. There were no exits now.

*   *   *

Whitney had never been approached before, not by an actual user, not like this. There was nothing to stop them from doing so, but generally they didn't, right? There were still such things as manners, and discretion, and at first she wanted to laugh at the absurd intrusion. His physical presence put her teeth on edge, too. He stood and moved as though a slightly larger human were inside his skinny frame, hunching him and bulging his eyes and making his fingers twitch; like everything inside him was trying to claw its way out. In a still photo, he might have looked normal, even attractive, but the reality of his body was one of barely concealed turmoil. The way he angled himself over her: it was abnormal, unsettling, as though he wanted to shield her from the rest of the bar, but not in a protective way. She felt invisible and alone and hated herself for it, reminded herself of the button in her jacket pocket, that she was free, at any moment, to say words to his face like *no* and *not interested*, that she didn't even owe him words and could simply turn her back. Although there were ways to do this that didn't engender conflict. Conflict had fatigued her enough. So, although she spat *coward* at herself in the gauntlet of her mind, she stayed, and thought.

It had started out okay, if unwanted. "Charlie," he had said, with an eagerness so palpable she could have bitten through it and spat out the center like a lump of fat in a steak. She had murmured something like *uh-huh*. Immediate wrongness, was her thought, the way he was staring down at her, the way his eyes seemed to open and then open, impossibly, again. It was something like intuition but not even that subtle: something like smelling smoke a block from your house, and then, with the logic of a nightmare, finding yourself trailing fire trucks home. And then, as if to confirm her fears, he had said what she had never heard before—never dreamt she'd hear, because in the real world, nobody would ever be so tactless as to come right up to you and say it. Shit wasn't supposed to work that way. "I'm a big fan," he said. Thankfully she didn't laugh, although she was close. She was also close to crying. To feel naked on camera was one thing. To feel naked in public when you were fully clothed: that was something else, a sensation laced with enough gall to give her that spirally nauseous feeling, hauntingly fresh, of being punched in the face.

The stuttery mouth, spit wet and with white teeth inside, was open and words were still coming out, but she wasn't listening; all her efforts were focused on edging away, so surreptitiously he might not notice, until she was out from his sinister sphere and could execute a graceful half-turn back to the bar, back to the safety of the known world. *Safety. The known world*: much later, after this night had been consigned to the pile of nights that had already happened to her, and that would keep happening to her, she would remember this thought and wonder why she'd suddenly decided the world was any safer than the man in front of her. Why she'd longed to turn back to the bar, leaning on wine-wet elbows on the glossy black surface, stretching her left leg out behind her with her shoe toe-grounded so her calf muscles popped.

Why she'd thought any of that was safe.

Rather than listen to anything he said, she found herself picturing herself as he must see her. As he must have seen her (and had her, and probably, now, was hitting play on her greatest hits in his mental video library). Bent over a couch in thong and garter belt and thigh-highs.

Standing, with one pensive hand on the window shade, naked from the waist down; a soft white sweater lapping at her shoulders, stilettos improbably hitched to her pale feet. Oh, she'd never actually entered the program to watch her own scenes—although she knew girls did, so they could self-castigate, so they could critique. Whitney, postfilming, had always tried to blank out these memories as fast as possible. It wasn't as if she was ashamed of her job. It had been, she told herself at the beginning, almost a philanthropic choice; there were so many people, nowadays, like the paraplegic and the bedridden and the cripplingly socially anxious, that had no other outlet. It seemed benign and humane, warm as a candy striper. And the money wasn't bad at all.

Though she did still block it out, just after filming, even though she kept telling herself it was for the right reasons. She blocked out the way she was told to arch her back, the way she was directed to wet her lips with a lazy tongue. She blocked out the legs spreading and the heavy-lidded glances and the slow unbuttoning of lacy bodysuits. Because living with that other person in her head, the one the rest of the world could meet whenever they wanted—could be with—it had proven very difficult.

She only knew herself. Whoever that other girl was, the one who left her image on the digital tracks at the AV department: She wasn't Whitney, exactly. She was like a Whitney costume, a Whitney costume that paid, and that, at the end of each days-long shoot, the real Whitney could unzip from, step out of, breathe. Have a well-deserved drink. Well. One a week, now. So, for sanity's sake, she blocked out what the Whitney costume did. But she hadn't actually blocked it out. Not really. All the memories were still there, and now, caught between this skinny dude in a pony-hair jacket and the wet dark bar, she rewatched them almost against her will, playing fast against the projector in her head. A thin scream banged its way up her esophagus. She swallowed some water and fought it back down, where she imagined the acids in her stomach seizing it with neon green hands and tearing it to bits. The urge hit again, the whiny siren begging her incessantly for fuel: beer, bourbon, anything to wash that taste of water from her throat.

*   *   *

Wasn't she lovely. Wasn't that a song, a song from long ago, one of those ballads the crooners dished out to sighing divorcees in old movies? *Isn't she lovely. Isn't she wonderful.*

Those were the only words he knew. They'd have to do. It seemed to be going well. She was looking up at him, her face tipped to catch the light, and a perfect storm of joy seized him as he saw, for real, the shadow of those eyelashes; the shadow he'd memorialized, in the darkness of his room, when he'd entered the program and found her in his bed. Because she always ended up in his bed, when he went inside the program. He sometimes tried out other girls; sometimes even brought them home; but they all left, readily enough, when he asked. This girl was different. Her name was, supposedly, Chandra. He had not yet figured out her real name. But he knew her, knew her with the certainty that he knew the timing of the flight paths that boiled over his house, the specificity with which he could time the weekly deliveries of his beer and toilet paper. He knew her because they'd known each other for a long time now.

Two or three nights a week, he strapped on his goggles, lay down carefully in bed, and entered the program. Within a few minutes he had always found her. It was like fate; it was like destiny slapping him in the face, how easy it was for him to cycle through the options, to pick the right staircase, to open the correct door, to see Chandra: reclining on a bed, in something diaphanous and golden. And then, like clockwork, he'd extend his hand to her. He'd bring her back to him. He'd have her right where he wanted her. He was telling her about the work he was doing with Ionic when he saw it. A girl at the other end of the bar, her red curls dripping down her shoulder blades, sharp-toned shoulders beckoning in tight chambray. She looked at him. She looked at him more. A smile curved her purple lips, one that seemed aimed not over his shoulder but directly to him. He sent her over a *who, me?* back. She beckoned, the tip of an index finger curling twice quickly back toward her body. He looked down at the girl crouched—crouched against the bar. Saucer eyes. Smile grim and plastered on. The wary, prowling nerves of a cobra, ready to spread its hood. There was nothing in this girl, whatever her name was, that reminded him of Chandra. Chandra was vital, sexy, condescending, sweet: whatever you wanted her to be, and whenever. She read your moods; she attuned herself to them. You could hold her down over the back of a chair and take her like a brute—or you could lower her into your soft bed, take her camisole straps off with your teeth, and she would hold your head and whisper things to you, things like *yes baby right there* and *don't stop.*

This—this was a hologram, some nothing he'd mistaken for his love. He abruptly backed away from her. She looked confused, then, with alacrity, her face loosened. Five years younger. Beautiful, he supposed, but nothing he could stand to talk to for one moment more.

He turned his back on her and went to find the redhead.

* * *

Safety. The known world. But nothing could explain the way these things occurred; by dint of being female and pretty and out in all of it, she seemed to welcome these instances, although they were as unwelcome to her as pneumonia or a pap smear. The known world was not safe. She knew this. But in certain ways, the way she held herself, for example, with her finger on the button in her jacket pocket; the way she always knew where the exits were; in some ways, the known world was as safe as it could be for someone like her. When the man backed away, a curtain abruptly dropping behind his face, she felt a hollow bliss. She had done nothing, had said nothing, and had somehow won. Although maybe it was not so much a victory as a standoff; maybe it was not about winning so much as it was about trying as hard as she could not to lose.

She walked home by herself that night in the mellow air, the prescribed two drinks melting quick and silent in her blood, and did not worry, although she kept her finger on the button in her jacket pocket. The encounter at the bar already felt like a dream: technicolor, and fast dissolving. How strange it was, that she could forget these things so swiftly after they happened. And they happened. Last December, outside Brimley's, being backed into the corner between the dumpster and the wall, stared at by a man exactly as tall as she was in her four-inch platforms, a man whose eyes she'd met time and again and convinced herself she'd read love there—shortly before jetting whiskey-spit aslant, he called her a succubus and grinned like a face behind a window in a horror movie. Then he left.

By now, she was far past the point of thinking she could read things in eyes, but if she'd still subscribed to that old false poetry, she would have said his eyes had something of the animal in them, something not hate so much as lizard-brained rage. Or. This April. Sideways shifting through a brimming, anxious crowd at the Ray Damien retrospective, her ass was grabbed by someone she was too trapped to turn around and identify—shaking herself away with a delayed reaction, bile boiling up her throat—and the whole rest of the night she'd found herself glaring at people she knew, wondering whether one of them had done it. In the car home the driver, whose profile said he was from Georgia-the-country-not-the-state, offered to slow down when he saw she was putting in her eyedrops. She'd said thanks but that it didn't matter. He'd watched as she walked to the door and didn't drive away until she was inside the vestibule, an act which she'd decided to take as a kindness.

*   *   *

Whitney's mother—back when she still took her daughter's calls, back before she'd messaged the entire family to officially "disown" Whitney (though if the flow of money in the family went in any direction, it would have gone from Whitney to her), a message spotted with words like *whore* and *disgrace*—had asked her once to tell her what anxiety felt like. The idea that someone could live *without* anxiety had been so alien to Whitney that she'd just laughed, and her mother had, with concern predominant in her breathy voice, asked her what she was laughing about. And then Whitney realized, her innards crashing together, that some people just didn't feel it: didn't know what it was like to live with a belt constantly tightening around your rib cage, or to wake up gasping for air because you'd stopped breathing in your sleep and your brain had decided to see if you were still alive. "It's like," she said, and then stopped, trying to figure out how to describe it to someone who didn't know. "It's like being constantly worried that you left the dog in the hot car, but you don't own a dog. Or a car."

Then it was her mother who'd laughed. "Honey," she said, as Whitney crushed the phone to her right shoulder, stepped into the bathroom, pulled her eyelids down, and looked in the mirror for signs of jaundice, seeing only the normal sleepless red-veined white. "That's not anxiety. That's just being a person." And Whitney didn't know what to say to that. A few months later she'd told her mother about her new job, in the AV department, one for which she'd beat out dozens of girls, one that would let her live in the city, one that would give her the time and money to figure out what it was she really needed to be. They hadn't talked much since.

STEPHANIE PUSHAW is a writer and editor from Los Angeles. She was a Truman Capote Fellow at the University of Montana, where she received an MFA in Fiction. Her short stories appear in Narrative, Sundog Lit, *and* Joyland, *and her essays in* Mississippi Review, DIAGRAM, *and* Los Angeles Review of Books. *Stephanie has also doctored screenplays, edited interviews for* The Believer, *and lived in eight cities on three continents (so far). She is currently a PhD candidate in Fiction at the University of Houston.*